William Sime

Haco the Dreamer

A Tale of Scotch University Life: Vol. II

William Sime

Haco the Dreamer
A Tale of Scotch University Life: Vol. II

ISBN/EAN: 9783337137069

Printed in Europe, USA, Canada, Australia, Japan

Cover: Foto ©Andreas Hilbeck / pixelio.de

More available books at **www.hansebooks.com**

HACO THE DREAMER

A Tale of Scotch University Life

BY

WILLIAM SIME

AUTHOR OF 'KING CAPITAL,' 'TO AND FRO,' 'THE RED ROUTE,' ETC.

IN TWO VOLUMES

VOL. II

London:

REMINGTON & CO., PUBLISHERS

HENRIETTA STREET, COVENT GARDEN

1884

CONTENTS

———

CHAPTER VIII

HACO THE DREAMER

CHAPTER I

ON THE FIRTH

HACO was dreadfully ashamed of himself after the grieve left him and strode across the field behind his daughter. He went down on the beach, and, sitting upon a boulder, he clasped his knees with his hands and gazed into space.

Why, had not Tree, the consummate artist, kissed Christie's landlady behind the door, and nobody had said a word—not even the very nearly Rev.

Mr Watson? The landlady herself had not said anything. He did not suppose that what a consummate artist might do with impunity should be denied to him. Of course Tibbie was different from Christie's landlady; she was out of sight prettier, and everything had led up to the circumstance as naturally as could be. He had read a poem to her, and her eyes had sparkled, and she looked as if she would have liked to have a poem written to her, too. A few changes of name, indeed, would have suited the poem to Tibbie's hair, face, and complexion, though she did not the least resemble Lady Mary; her honest red hands not being at all like Lady Mary's. If he had only thought of it in time, he might have given the poem to Tibbie, with a few changes of name. But then there was the grieve and his inexorable wrath— the good, friendly Mr Baxter, who had been so kind to him all his life, and who, all of a sudden, had been transformed to an enemy. Really, it seemed as if he were destined to please nobody, and the thought which struck him beside Mons Meg came back to him again. He would go away and drown himself. Perhaps he might meet his mother again when he was drowned; at any rate, he could not possibly meet anybody or anything more inexorable than the grieve, if he did strip himself of his life.

Yet, after all, as he went on thinking about it, here were the birds singing in the rear of him, the sun warming the beach at his elbow, and his yacht launched ready for a sail into the North Sea, if he cared to take it. To be sure, he cared; he would go up to the grieve's, renew his promise to Mr Baxter, and ask Sandy to accompany him. Yes; there was a light breeze shimmering on the surface of the Firth; it was high time he were afloat. He would go up to the Manor and put on his yachting gear, then he would see Sandy and carry him off.

Sandy was out at the time Haco approached the Mains, so was his father, as he was very glad to hear from Mrs Baxter, who received him with a bright smile and a long grasp of his hand.

'Eh, well, now, Mr Haco, you're not so strong-looking, after your session, as you should be. You've been working too hard. Come away in and sit down.'

Haco saw Sandy's medals on the mantelpiece, and sighed as he sat down.

'No; I'm sure I haven't overworked myself. You don't catch me coming back with any of these things, Mrs Baxter. I've got nothing.'

'Oh, but you're young yet. You have plenty of time before you.'

'So has Sandy.'

'He hasn't so much time as you, for a grieve's

son maun work for his bread. You have it all made for you, ready baked, Mr Haco. It's a great difference, at all times.'

'I didn't think of that,' said Haco. 'Your fowls are looking in fine condition, Mrs Baxter. What a bantam, to be sure! Where did you get him? A bantam and his wife! What a regular little randy! How he crows, to be sure! —with a rapidity and a decision worthy of a more important fowl.'

'He rules the farmyard,' said Mrs Baxter. 'He'll come in, if I ask him. Tuck, tuck, tuck! tuck, tuck, tuck! teukie, teukie, teukie!'

The bantam, lifting his heels with a contemplative air, slowly entered, followed by his wife, who devoured all the corn thrown down by Mrs Baxter.

'He's for a' the world like a wee popular lord,' said Mrs Baxter. 'Look at the way he hauds his head! Tuck, tuck, tuck! teukie, teukie, teukie!'

'You're for the sea?' said Mrs Baxter, starting the conversation again, which was interrupted by a sorrowful expression coming over Haco's face.

'Yes. But do you know, Mrs Baxter, I'm awfully sorry. I've offended Mr Baxter deeply. I never offended anybody as much. I don't think he'll ever speak to me again. And I always used to like him so much.'

'Wheesht!' said Mrs Baxter. 'Tibbie tauld me. She's a bold, thoughtless girl, and I've given her my mind. I know that you never meant anything whatever. Do I no mind, mysel?' she continued, wiping her mouth. 'Ay, well that! You see they've made Alexander an elder, and he's ta'en up wi' serious notions; not but what he's right in some part of them. But he should discriminate. Dinna you fash. And Alexander, he'll never think o't again. Here's Sandy. Sandy, this is Mr Haco, wanting you to take a sail.'

'Where's Tibbie?' asked Sandy, in a gloomy

accent, holding out his hand to Haco. 'Spens, you've made my father very angry,' he said.

Mrs Baxter lifted her hands with some surprise. Here was Sandy calling the laird's son by his last name. Then she looked at the medals on the mantelpiece, and felt that her son was justified in calling anybody anything, She had heard him allude to Sir Thomas himself as 'Old Free Incisions,' that very day, and she looked out of the window to see if the sky was falling; but the sky didn't fall. 'Spens' and 'Old Free Incisions!' Well, well, she mentally agreed with her husband's comprehensive summary of surprise, 'Od's sake! I do *not* know what the world's coming to.'

'See,' she continued, averting her son's seriousness, ' here's your auld oilskin. Go away down to the shore with Mr Spens and get your sail.'

Sandy put an oilskin over his arm and followed Haco, who exclaimed,

'I wish people didn't take things so seriously.'

The pungent sea breeze blowing freely over the fields soon worked all the seriousness out of Sandy's mind.

By the time they had reached the shore he had forgotten about Tibbie and his outraged dignity as her brother. He was quite prepared to throw himself into his sail with full enjoyment, and while Haco ran over to the Manor to get fishing lines and something from Isaac to eat, Sandy went on board and got out a jib and fore-sail.

Haco rushed over the shingle and joined him, his arm full of lines and 'grub,' as he called his lunch.

'She's beginning to strain at her anchor already,' cried Haco. 'We can get out with a jib and fore-sail, Sandy. Wait a minute till I come aboard, before you hoist the mainsail. There's a big breeze coming in from the mouth of the Firth. We'll cut across to Cramond in no time, or it'll—— Don't drop the lines. I say, Sandy, I don't feel like a man a bit. I feel every bit as young as I was before I went to the University—don't you?'

'I'm older than you,' said Sandy, seriously, hauling away at the anchor chain. 'There's too much sunlight, man, for us to get any fish. They'll not take with all that sunshine upon the water. They'll see the hooks.'

'Oh, rather! Yes, I should think they would see the hooks. We haven't got a morsel of bait— not a single herring, mussel, cockle, or limpet. I saw a lot of fish drying outside the garden wall, Sandy. You might—— Well, no; let's toss for it. I mean, you know, that it's your turn to go for something. I went for the lines and the lunch. But let's toss. Heads or tails, Sandy?'

'Tails,' said Sandy, with a rope in his teeth and his hands still on the chain.

'Heads it is. No, it isn't; the half crown's come down sideways. I'll make it the best of three. Heads or tails, Sandy?'

' Tails it is this time,' said Sandy.

' Yes, but it's best of three. This shot decides it. We stand at one to me and one to you. Heads or tails, Sandy ? '

'Tails.'

' You go for the bait. Heads it is. You'll find a cod or something drying just outside the wall. Bring the whole of him, and never mind Isaac or anybody if he looks over the garden wall and says " Hey, leave that alone, will ye ! " You might double up as you go under the wall, in case anybody does see you and make a row.'

Haco watched Sandy going along the walk outside the wall. He looked preternaturally innocent, and did not double up as he had been advised. On the contrary, he looked over the wall, and began conversing with somebody. No doubt it was Isaac. At the same time he dropped his oilskin over a cod, and, stooping, lifted both at once without interrupting his conversation with Isaac, who evidently suspected nothing.

'After all, Sandy's a very good fellow in spite of his medals,' reflected Haco, when he saw him sauntering back with his booty, while Isaac's head appeared at the wall looking after him.

'Plenty of bait there, Sandy,' said Haco, bringing the cod on board and settling himself at the tiller, having fastened the sheet of the main-sail and seen Sandy seated at the fore-sail.

The breeze played softly on them as long as they were within the lee of the land, but the gurgle of the water had no sooner begun at the bows than Haco roared,

'We are Vikings, Sandy—Vikings from over the seas! Hang the hospitals, and the class-rooms, and the degrees! What do you think of them now?'

'Oh, this is well enough,' said Sandy, peering beneath the sail. 'Starboard a little, Spens; as soon as we are out we will have a smashing

breeze. Keep your seat. She'll heel over to the
water's edge before she starts off up the Firth.
You're off for Cramond are you and the Queensferry direction?'

'Starboard it is, you prosy fellow. You decline
to become a Viking. I say, this is a stiffish breeze.
Glorious little Spray! How she dips her head into
it! Yes, it is high time you put that water-
proof over you. You must be drenched with
that first dip. Come further aft.'

The little yacht soon responded to the singing of
the wind among her cordage. Having felt the free
sweep of the breeze, she dipped her bow once, twice,
thrice, right into the waves, threw off a white surge
or two, and rushed up the Firth.

As they passed Binkie Manor, Isaac was shading
his eyes on a garden walk, and Sandy declared he
saw Sir Thomas looking at them out of a window.

'Steady, Spens. Bring her out a little; here's a
coaster from Alloa who won't move for us. I say,

we'll come very close to hitting her. Hang them! they're taking the wind out of our sails Now the sea is free before us all the way to Cramond. Nothing but solan geese and seagulls.'

'I believe, notwithstanding your dogmatic assertion, that we shall have some very good fishing, Sandy.'

The sky was blue above them. Only here and there were there icebergs of white cloud sailing, as the Spray sailed, swift and stately through the celestial sea overhead.

'Sandy,' cried Haco, looking up from his tiller 'what are you and I after all, but a couple of fish in the bottom of that deep sea, the atmosphere? I don't know much chemistry; but all the difference between air and sea seems to me that the sea is thicker than the air, only another sort of air and moveable land, as it were, where they can feed and breathe, the cod, and ling, and flounders, and trout, and salmon, and seal, and whale.'

'Port!' cried Sandy, looking at a rush of wind which swept over the waves, as if a league of invisible wings was hastening towards them, casting a black shadow on the blue of the sea.

'Port it is!' called Haco, as the yacht heeled to the sea. 'Thank Heaven for a deep keel! If we were crank we should founder. How we spin along!'

'It'll take us two or three hours to come back, if this wind doesn't lift,' cried Sandy.

'Oh, never mind the hours. Who cares for the hours, or time, or eternity, or anything but the breeze, and the sea, and the sunshine, and the violet sky? Port! yes, all right. I am going straight in on the red target of the artillerymen, then we will sweep the coast and throw out an anchor opposite Cramond. Perhaps we will go up and look at Barnbogle. D'ye know, I rather like that ivy-covered ruin on the shore. I am going to write a poem about it. Would you like to hear the plot of it? I say, Sandy, come further aft; there's no necessity for you getting all that spray. Here's a flask for you and some sherry. Don't take it all. Listen to me singing a song.'

And Haco broke out with—

> ' At the castell of Edinbruch,
>> Upon the bank baith green and rough,
>>> As mine alone I lay,
>> With paper, pen, and ink in hand,
>> Musing, as I could understand
>>> Of the sudden decay
>> That unto this puir nation
>>> Appearandly does come ;
>> I fand our congregation
>>> Was cause of all and some ;
>> Wha's actors, instructors,
>>> Has blinded them sae lang,
>> That blameless, and shameless,
>>> Baith rich and puir they wrang.'

' Helm down!' shouted Sandy.

> 'But the great God Omnipotent, (sang Haco),
>> That secret thoughts does pierce,
>> Relieved has that innocen'.
>>> Out of their rage sae fierce ;
>> Provided and guided
>>> Her to an uncouth land,
>> Where wander and slander
>>> With enemies nane she fand.'

' It's a bonny bit ballad, too,' said Sandy. ' But

if you run in too close you'll be ashore, an' we'll have to swim for't.'

> 'Thus syled, beguiled (sang Haco),
>   They will but get the glaiks ;
> Come they here, thir twa year,
>   They sall not miss their paiks.'

'Mind that roller, Spens! Duck! Hold on! That was a narrow shave.'

> 'Sae muse them '——

sang Haco, dripping from the wash of a wave which had gone from stem to stern.

> 'Sae muse them and chuse them,
>   What part they will ensue ;
> Forsake them, or back me,
>   They sall drink as they brew.'

Sandy crawled aft and brought down the main-sail; he had already reefed the jib and fore-sail.

'Now, out with the anchor; we've got right into a flock of seagulls, and will catch no end of fish. That's the River Almond coming out over there. If the tide was high, we might run up and get a bannock at the inn. Off goes the anchor!'

'There's no bottom to it,' said Haco; 'we'll drift.

Never mind ; tear up the cod, bait the hooks, and trust in Providence.'

'Trust in Providence! Ay, ay,' said Sandy; 'when the anchor's got a hold I'll begin to think about it.'

'Sandy, I believe you're a regular Davie Hume. You don't believe in anything but facts. It's my opinion that Scots haven't an ounce of belief among them, from the Tweed to John o' Groats, for all that they go on about kirks and all that.'

'Have you a sinker on your line?' asked Sandy.

'Yes, as much lead as would roof Binkie. Oh, confound it, Sandy! before I have my line in you have brought up a fish—a great, white, fat brute. What is it? Sandy, I wish you would help me to take the hooks out of the ravel. They're all mixed up. You'll exhaust the bank before I start at all.'

'Hey,' said Sandy, impatiently, passing over his own line to Haco, and unravelling and baiting his hooks in the twinkling of an eye.

'Another fish, Sandy: I say, this is rather slow work. Let's change places. They seem all to have got to your side.'

'Change away,' said Sandy, pulling in fish after fish, while Haco brought up his hook time after time without anything on it.

'Sandy,' he said, when the latter had covered the deck with whitings, while he had caught none, 'I don't think I am of any use in the world.'

'You dinna need to be,' said Sandy, sardonically.

CHAPTER II

LADY MARY

LADY MARY HAY sat at breakfast in Great King Street. She was arrayed in a light morning-gown, which took from her the appearance of the nursing sister. She was sipping coffee and reading a poem. It was Haco's anonymous effusion which had reached her by that post. She saw through it at once. She saw through his disguised handwriting. She understood the allusions to her work in the wards; she smiled at the terse expressions of adoration ; she sighed as she smiled, and laid down her admirer's verses.

'Poor boy!' said Lady Mary, 'his heart is not in his work. I am afraid he will have to change if he is to step into his father's reputation. He is a poet, I greatly fear. Unhappy boy! And yet how delicate his compliments are! how musical! I hope —I hope, poor boy, he is not in love.'

Lady Mary was about Haco's age, but she had more experience of the world. She had been greatly persecuted by lovers. She did not much like love-making. It seemed to her that life was too serious for dalliance. With so many blind, and halt, and lame on her mind, she could not respond to the ardour of those who had approached her with compliment. It was affectionate persecution which had driven her, at last, to decide to attach herself to a ward. But Haco's affection did not disturb her.

'I think a poem a good safety-valve,' said her

ladyship, again taking it up and reading it, with great deliberation, first to herself, then aloud; 'a good safety-valve,' she said, locking it away in an escritoire.

She then sat down and wrote a note to Haco. 'It will,' she reflected, 'be better that the poor boy should know that I understand where the poem came from. It will save him from illusion. He must know how I regard it. "Dear Mr Spens," she began, and promptly tore up the sheet of paper, emblazoned with the Strawfield arms—a rick of hay, with a rake leaning on it. "Dear Haco," she resumed, and again tore up her paper. Then she unfolded the poem, spread it out in front of her, and rapidly wrote off:

'MY DEAR HACO—This is a very charming way you have taken to remind me of your existence. The poem you have addressed to me is at once melodious and strong. The expressions of ardent

attachment I take to be addressed to some being
of your imagination. I, at least, have not the
pleasure of her acquaintance, but should suppose
that she must be very good and beautiful from
what you say of her. I shall be at Farmline one
of these days, and may make it convenient to call
on Sir Thomas. I think of going to Vienna for
a little. I fear there is no chance of our Scotch
University seeing its way to opening its doors for
the suppliants. In Vienna we can obtain degrees
and practise our profession. You see, my views
have enlarged themselves since I saw you last.
Then I was content to be a nursing sister; now
I am content with nothing short of being a recognised expert in the line I have taken up. Sir
Thomas' advice will be invaluable to me in this
new undertaking.'

Then she put the poem away again, and sat
down to stare into the fire. Lady Mary's pulses

had been stirred by the unequal contest which the ladies who wished to become doctors had waged with the University. She felt herself so competent to discharge well all the duties of a doctor, that she sympathised heart and soul with those who clamoured for admittance at the University gates, but who were elbowed out by a jealous professorate. Yes, she would make herself one with them in their aims; but, instead of staying in Edinburgh to fight the reluctant professors, she would go to Vienna, graduate, and undertake what work she liked, and where she thought it was most wanted.

'That silly boy!' she repeated, going to her escritoire and again unfolding the poem, 'he means me, I suppose. He lavishes on me all his adjectives. He is—yes, he is in love with me. Silly, silly, boy!' But Lady Mary put her lips to it before she fastened it away, out of sight; and all that morning she thought of nothing but Haco Spens.

CHAPTER III

SKETCHING

NOTHING of importance occurred during Haco's holidays till the very end of them. He spent his month at the Manor in the most enjoyable way. He forgot his difficulties on that golden shore, passing with Sandy a large part of his time on the water. They made schemes for their coming session. Haco was to co-operate with Sandy. The latter did not need to take botany and zoology—they were not included in the extra-mural course; but he determined to take them with a view to passing the M.B. examination at the London University later on, so that the pair should do a large portion of their work in common.

'See if I don't beat you,' said Haco, 'in fair competition.'

'I would like to cut in on a couple of University medals,' said Sandy; 'it would keep up the prestige of the extra-mural. I know my professors would like me to run away with a botany or zoology medal.'

'You'll not find it so easy, with three or four hundred fellows in a class, to run away with a medal. It's not exactly the same thing as competing with one's self, you know, Sandy.'

'No,' said Sandy, who busied himself, more or less, all the recess, with making dissections of mice and fish, and in pulling the petals out of flowers; while Haco lay much on his back, and watched the clouds floating overhead in the sea of blue.

He obeyed his father's injunctions literally, and
not only did not speak of medicine, but even suc-
ceeded in driving most thoughts about it from his
mind.   But he went on reading irrelevant volumes
of poetry and building up castles in the air, which
were not, perhaps, meant to stand the cold blasts
which would blow upon them from the world of
real life.   That did not hinder Haco's building
them, however, as he listened to the sounds of
melody which floated round the Manor.   The event
which occurred towards the end of the recess was
the appearance one morning of Eli Tree upon the
beach of one of the little bays, his easel mounted
with a large piece of canvas, and a picture growing
under his hand, representing the wild rolling of
the surf upon the shingle, a bit of background in
which the gnarled roots of the trees were represented twisting themselves into the bank in
serpentine coils.   Haco was surprised and delighted
to see his friend.   He knew that many of his

canvases had been taken from that shore. But to
see him actually at work on one of the Binkie
bays, it made Haco run along the shingle and
grasp his hand with tremendous fervour.

'I say, my young cock,' said Tree, 'you'll get
over that habit of shaking hands—gripping a
fellow's hand as if yours were a vice. Your
perfervidum ingenium will cool a little when you
have shaken as many hands as I have.'

'I am sorry my cordiality offends you, Tree.
I only meant to welcome you to our sea-coast.
Besides, I'm awfully glad to see your good blowzy
face and jolly appearance.'

'When you have shaken as many hands as I
have, Spens,' proceeded Tree, 'the offensive hand-
shake of persons who imitate the Freemason
signs, so as to make a shilling or two; the hand-
shake, prolonged like the working of a pump, of
people who don't care a rap if you drop dead at
their feet; the wibbledy-wobbledy shake of the

fatuous; the shake of the indifferent, which is no shake, but only a closing of the fingers; the patronizing shake of the cad, who puts out one digit, and expects no foot to be raised in reply '——

' I say, Tree, you are about as eloquent as poor Mr Watson, that you turned out of Christie's that night.'

' Then I say, my young friend, that you will acquire the habit of making a moderate, reasonable shake go a long way. It commits you to nothing, and performs all the office of cordiality required from one man to another when he meets him.'

' Well, I'm sorry I was so familiar, Tree. I didn't mean it. I won't do it again. Give me your hand again, and let me practise this new, chilly, decorous shake that you recommend.'

Haco took Tree's hand, and gripping it, went over all the shakes in turn.

'Now, that's about enough, Spens. What have you been doing with your holidays?'

'Not much. Lying out on the Firth for the week past. You see my little Spray anchored out there; we can run her—Sandy and I—with a good steady wind, as fast as a screw. I love her as if she were a life, and shall be sorry to leave her behind.'

'Why should you leave her behind? There's plenty o' room in Granton Harbour for a thing o' that sort. I know some men who go down there from Edinburgh and spend a day on the water now and again. There's nothing to hinder it.'

'Tree, you're a genius. That's precisely what I'll do. I'll have her taken over to Granton Harbour, and get a sail now and then. I say, there's an idea for you! I know Lady Mary puts her carriage at the disposal of some of the children from her ward, and drives them out to the Pentland Hills now and again. Why shouldn't

I lend them my yacht, and take them down to the
Bass Rock ?   I believe Lady Mary would come too.
Tree, I never thought of it before.   That's exactly
what I'll do.   It would do some of those poor pale-
faced children no end of good.'

'Yes, it might spoil them for practical life, and
if there was anything of a sea on the Firth, it
might make their faces a degree paler.'

'I can't make you out, Tree.   You make a happy
suggestion one moment, and withdraw it the next.
But, by the way, talking of Lady Mary Hay, she's
coming to Binkie to-day.   I shouldn't wonder if
she were on her way now.'

'You're mighty fond of talking about Lady Mary
Hay,' said Tree, resuming his brush and dashing at
the canvas. 'There you are, now,' he said. 'There's
that seagull caught at the moment he was turning
to the sun, with the glint on his wing thrown in
exactly as it flashed out there.'

'I don't know how you do it, Tree.   If I were

dashing at the canvas that way, I should only make a smudge. It really is, now, an exquisite bit of painting. Father will want to buy that, I'm convinced. I know he bought a view up among the fields one day from an artist he knew nothing about, and who had no reputation whatever.'

'You mean that, like me, perhaps he wasn't an Associate or an Academician. That sometimes means, my boy, that an artist is a bad diplomatist, and doesn't know how to pull the tea-party wire to advantage.'

'It's lunch time. Suppose you come up with me and take this with us. I'll try and get father to buy it. What would you think it worth?'

'As much as the scene itself is worth. No money can buy it. The waves are rolling there; the roots are twisting there; the gull's wings are glinting there, under my hand, as they are rolling, twisting, and glinting under the hand of the Creator in the scene itself.'

'Still, I suppose you must sell your pictures.'

'It's a mere side issue,' said Tree. 'It has nothing to do with the creation.'

'Come along, then. I'll carry it very carefully.'

The pair went over the rocks and ascended the garden walks, and in front of the Manor found Lady Mary Hay and Sir Thomas Spens pacing to and fro. They were in close, earnest conversation ; Sir Thomas apparently expostulating—Lady Mary defending her position with quiet self-restraint. Tree was struck with her ladyship's appearance.

'I understand,' he said 'why it's always Lady Mary this, and Lady Mary that; and Lady Mary used to say, and Lady Mary thinks, and I'll ask Lady Mary. Hang it! I'll have her in a foot or two of canvas before I leave you. I like that masterly quietness and subdued dignity.'

They came up to the front of the house, Haco carrying Tree's picture at arm's length. His arm trembled a little as Lady Mary looked at him, and

he felt the blood mount in confusion to his brow.
He was not able at once to shake hands with her ;
nor could he unceremoniously put down Tree's
scene, in case of an abrupt expression of opinion
from that worthy calculated to shock the ears of
Lady Mary.

' Well,' said Sir Thomas, a little hastily—he had
evidently been arguing a disagreeable question—
' who's your friend, Haco ? '

' Mr Eli Tree,' said Haco, looking affectionately
at Lady Mary, and seeming to feel the weight of
her letter, which reposed in his breast pocket.

' Eh ? ch ? ' said Sir Thomas, with a mixture of
approval and alarm. He had heard of Tree's
pictures ; but he had also heard of his antics, and,
as he believed that evil communications corrupt
good manners, he was not as cordial as he might
have been. But Lady Mary smiled on him, and
said,

' Mr Tree, we have one of your exquisite land-

scapes at Strawfield. Whenever I wished to feel
the large atmosphere of the shore and the sea,
I looked at it and felt refreshed.'

'I'm always pleased to know that my work is
appreciated,' said Tree, in a sturdy, downright
voice. 'I remember the picture you allude to.
I recollect selling it to your brother, the earl, on
the sea-shore, just as I want to sell this to you
now, Sir Thomas Spens. Throw the shadow on
it, Haco. Not so much. No, get out of the line
of the sun. There you are, sir. What d'ye say
now? Once, twice, thrice—eh? what d'ye say,
Sir Thomas?'

Lady Mary looked a little shocked; so was
Haco, who wished Tree would not adopt quite so
strong an auctioneering tone.

Sir Thomas looked keenly at the picture.

'Some of my brother surgeons are better judges
than I am; but that's a very fair rendering, Mr
Tree, of one of my nooks on the shore. I don't

dislike it; but as to purchasing it, that's quite a different matter. I have a good deal of water-colour and oil about the Manor—chiefly presents, however, which cost me nothing.'

'I never make presents,' said Tree, a little contemptuously.

'What do you value it at?' asked the baronet.

'I'll take your cheque for two hundred and fifty pounds, if you please.'

'What!' said Sir Thomas. 'I'll be bound to say that is paying yourself at the rate of twenty-five shillings a minute.'

'It's paying myself at the rate of thirty shillings a minute, if you like to take that view of it. But will you please to remember the bitter long years of privation and slavery I went through before I could paint you or any other man this picture? Two hundred and fifty pounds, sir, or nothing.'

'Do buy it, father. Tree can get anything he likes for it on the other side of the water.'

' Here, Isaac,' cried Sir Thomas, suddenly, caught by the new light thrown upon the picture and the glint of the gull's wings. ' Take this and place it carefully on the frame at the side of my study fire. We'll think about the purchase afterwards. If you are like me, Mr Tree, you will consider that money is no part of your professional consideration. For my own part, I regard my surgical operations as priceless. They have no equivalent in coin.'

' Yes,' said Tree, ' that's how I look at it, too. There are kinds of work, like yours and mine, Sir Thomas, which have no equivalent in money; but, for all that, I always insist on having my price.'

Lady Mary had walked off with Haco. Sir Thomas followed his newly-acquired picture into the house. Tree stood looking down over the sea towards Edinburgh; then his eye lighted on the boy and girl, as he thought them.

'It looks very like love,' he said. 'And pretty love-making it will be between such a pair. That gay young fellow, with as much knowledge of life as a calf, and the Lady Mary concealing under a sweet demeanour plenty of important knowledge of it. I'll ask them to oblige me. I say, my man,' addressing Isaac, who came to the door, with no visible intention of doing anything, 'if you'll go down the garden and over the rocks to the bay you saw on my canvas, you'll come to a portfolio and a box of pigments. Bring them round this way, will you?—I'm going to paint.'

'I never leave the house,' said Isaac. 'It's not my province to leave the house. We're all very satisfied with your picture.'

'That's very good o' you, now,' said Tree, touching his hat with mock humility. 'Get a hold o' somebody whose province it is to leave the house. Oh, you're interested in the young couple, are you?

That's what you came to look at ! What's old Bolus doing ?'

'Sir Thomas is searching for his cheque-book,' said Isaac, with marked dignity of utterance.

'Then, my good fellow, run along for those things that I left on the sea-shore, or '——

And Tree made a very good imitation of the growl of a tiger—so good, in fact, that Isaac instantly returned to the house and despatched a smart boy in buttons for the implements of the artist.

'Those are glass eyes,' said Tree, 'you have in your head, I suppose ?' as Isaac leant up against the doorway and scrutinized the rocky spot where Haco and Lady Mary had disappeared. 'The one nearest me is glass anyhow, and a precious lot of bottle-green in it, too. Oh, yes, they're both glass. A wonderful fellow old Spens! Don't you feel them rather heavy in your head, now?—like a couple of marbles, for example. Pity the poor blind man!'

Isaac curled his lips contemptuously as he looked at the 'mad painter,' and banged the door with considerable velocity.

Tree descended the garden, took his implements from the boy who had gone for them, and set out in search of Lady Mary and Haco.

Haco was sitting on the parapet wall at the foot of the garden, and Lady Mary was talking to him in an earnest voice.

'Sorry to interrupt you,' said Tree; 'but I want a loan of an attitude for a few minutes. I am sure your ladyship has enough of good-nature to oblige me by sitting on that wall, with Haco's arm round your waist.'

Haco frowned upon Tree; the Lady Mary turned and, with great sweetness, said,

'There are some requests I shall grant to no one on earth. That is one of them.'

'Give me the honour of a sitting, Lady Mary Hay, in any attitude you like, with or without Haco Spens?'

'I would rather not,' said Lady Mary.

'It would put me under eternal obligation.'

'That's a long period to carry a debt of gratitude for a trifle.'

'A trifle be it then, Lady Mary. Please to regard it as that, and let me have you as Youth at the prow and Pleasure at the helm,'

'Tree, you have no constructive genius out of landscape.'

'As youth at the prow, if you please, Lady Mary' Yes, thanks; by sitting a couple of yards apart from Spens, you give sufficient space for an imaginary boat. Youth, yes; Pleasure at the helm. Take your seat, Spens, as you would in your own pleasure-boat. Now, Pleasure! now, Youth! a fair wind to you, and a long voyage; and, Youth,

not so sad—not so sad! Pleasure, not so elated.
There, going, once—going twice—Youth at the
prow and Pleasure at the helm. It's a masterpiece
Now, you don't want me any longer.'

CHAPTER IV

BACK TO COLLEGE

Haco returned to Edinburgh in low spirits. The afternoon he had spent with Lady Mary was, indeed, a memory worth having. He thought he could survive upon it for a considerable time; but what made him miserable was that he would be obliged, after the summer session was over, so to survive.

Lady Mary had made up her mind to leave the angry turmoil of agitation which had set in upon the ladies who wished to study at Edinburgh, and

to betake herself to Vienna, where a diploma was
open to her, if she could win it. Sir Thomas had
urgently represented to her that she was giving
up the splendid privileges of her womanhood by
attempting to enter a field consecrated to men.
He had used all the arguments in his repertory,
but only to find that Lady Mary seemed more
and more determined to go to Vienna and get her
degree. She was still, however, to abide by the
hospital for the summer months. But the prospect of her going abroad seemed to rob Edinburgh of all its attractions for Haco. He went
back to his rooms in Queen Street, disheartened.
He thought they smelt musty. He found Mrs
Ramsay's greetings a little offensive in their
effusiveness. The bitter hours of the winter
seemed to hang about the window-curtains and
to pervade the furniture.

Three letters on the mantelpiece, in Roger
Thorburn's hand, completed the disenchantment

of his return to liberty; for on opening them he discovered that one of them contained a reminder of money due for the dead man's widow. Another one emphasized the statement and suggested a menace. The third announced that if the weekly instalments were not paid, recourse would be had by the friends of the murdered one to the machinery of the law.

Along with the letters, Roger enclosed a pamphlet by himself, called *Post Obitum*. It was a singular little treatise, composed for the benefit of invalids, and, to Haco's amazement he saw the letters M.D., LL.D., after the quack's name.

He then knew that he had executed his threat, and applied to the little Dutchman who obtained quack degrees for five pounds a-piece.

The same day he went up to the quadrangle of the University. It was very unlike the busy winter months. There were no art students, with their shining, morning faces; no law students, beginning

to look cynical, because of the foretaste of a knowledge of human character; no divinity students
carrying their heads high, with the conviction that
they might lecture crowned heads from pulpits
and be themselves not a pin the worse.

It was the summer session, and that belonged
to the medical students. The others, as I have
said, had all gone home; the poorer ones to work
on farms, to wait in hotels, to go out in fishing-
boats, to teach, to preach, to do anything which
would turn over enough of money to enable them
to come up smiling next session; the richer ones to
daudle at home, to spend five months in Berlin or
Heidelberg, or otherwise wait through the long
vacation for their next spell of reading.

Haco found the absence of variety in the faces a
new source of *ennui*. They were all men carrying
Quains under their arms, most of them having an
imitative resemblance to this or that professor
whom they admired. They were more or less all

pocket editions of Dr Crum, or Dr Dale, or Dr John, or Dr Joiner. There was even the unremoved whiff of mortality which clung to the garments of the dissectors and operators.

Haco did not remain long in the quadrangle after he had matriculated. He did not even go into the library, for fear he might see Roger and be pressed to a settlement of that abominable debt. Nor would he accompany a little batch of matriculators who asked him to go with them to Rutherford's. Rather he would go back to Queen Street and have his humble chop underdone. He was struck with the different aspect of the faces he met on the streets. Every other man was a parson. He wondered at first if some large funeral were collecting, to which so many men in black swallows and white 'chokers' were flocking. Who could it be? Going into a shop to buy the photographs of the professors of zoology and botany, he asked the man behind the counter

what was going on that so many, men wearing
black coats, were ebbing and flowing about the
street.

'These are the country ministers, man, in for the
Assemblies. A shilling a-piece for the professors of
botany and zoology. That's a very good likeness
of "Vascular Tissue"—they never call him anything else. That's a very fair representation of
"Bathybius," too—that's the only name he gets
over this counter. Familiarity, they say, breeds
contempt; but I've never heard these men called
anything else, and they're as much respected as
any men in the metropolis. It doesn't do a
professor much harm to call him "Bathybius,"
or "Vascular Tissue," or what you like. Would
you not like to buy the photograph of "Old
Free Incisions?"—a great man like Sir Thomas
Spens should be in the hand of every student
with a shilling to spare.'

'Is that my father you are talking about?' asked Haco.

'Are you a son of Sir Thomas'? Well, imitate him, then. Imitate him, and you'll be a credit to your country. I sell more photographs of Sir Thomas in a week than I do of "Vascular Tissue" in a year. Ah, you'll be a student at the science classes! Here's a book, now, written by a very clever fellow—a student like yourself—maybe a few years older—out of the notes he took from "Vascular Tissue's" lectures. Everything that "Tissue" has to say you'll find in these notes— a fine cramming book. If you'll buy a Liddell and Scott and a Dr Kitto, I'll give you these notes for nothing.'

'That's very good of you,' said Haco, lighting a cigar; 'but I have a Liddell already. I shouldn't think "Tissue" would care for your boning his lectures. They say they are rather "potty" lectures, at the best.'

'On the contrary,' said the shopkeeper, 'he likes it. He has now a European reputation.'

'Did he not have that before?'

'Hardly. Here's another caird of your father— a better one than you have purchased.'

'No, thanks; I mustn't spend any more money.'

In the street nothing but country ministers—men who looked as if they had a superb ignorance of the world and fine digestions. As they met each other they often stopped and shook hands—not in the temperate manner recommended by Tree, but with a fervid grasp, which seemed to betoken a long course of friendship, suppressed by absence. They guffawed, too, in the open air, and thundered their remarks, and seemed to make themselves greatly at home on the pavements of the metropolis. The more elegant and well-dressed pastors frequented the Princes Street hotels. He saw the parish minister of Binkie come out of one, wiping his lips, so he concluded they must be Established

Church men. He noticed the more devout and un-
worldly in appearance go into temperance hotels—
among them the Free Church minister of Binkie—
so he judged these to be members of the Free
Church. The U.P. minister of Binkie he saw
ascending an omnibus, eating a mutton-pie like
Sandy's father, followed by four other pastors
eating 'cookies.' They seemed to be going home
to lodgings, so Haco made up his mind that they
all belonged to the U.P. Church. It was his first
lesson in ecclesiastical polity. He sat down to his
chop, underdone, with *Post Obitum* before him.
Then he fell asleep, and did not awaken till far on
in the evening, when he remembered it was time
for him to go up and see Sandy Baxter.

It was dark when he had gone along Nicolson
Street to the lane which led to Salisbury Street.
When he reached it, he heard Sandy's voice ex-
claiming,

'Oh, Robert! you must lay down your end of

it for a little. I must take a breath. It's dreadfully heavy.'

Then Sandy stood panting audibly, while he
deposited the end of a huge chest. The man at
the other end of it grumbled, and said he had as
much pith in his 'pinkey' as Sandy in his whole
body. Haco recognized him as the policeman who
had appeared at Christie's.

'Good gracious, Sandy! what are you carrying?' asked Haco. 'I was coming along to see
you.'

'It's my trunk,' said Sandy. 'That confounded
landlady of mine! I left a pot of jam when I
went home, and she says she washed it out. I
had a couple of ounces of tea in a caddy, and she
says she doesn't know anything about it. And
the remains of my meal are all gone; the window
was open, and the meal—there was so little of it—
got all blown about the floor one day with a wind
coming down Arthur's Seat. I suspected her

before I left; but now I'm sure of it, though she's a very plausible character.'

'He's a wee thing hard, and that's the fact,' said the policeman, who was helping him to carry his trunk. 'I get on with her fine.'

'I daresay. You've all the law at your back. But I'm a defenceless object, and I will not be cheated.'

'Dinna be too anxious not to be cheated,' said the policeman, taking out a red handkerchief and wiping his brow. 'There's a time o' life when it's better for a person to be cheated. Take a little of it, and never let on you see it.'

'That's what they call "salad days," isn't it, bobby?' asked Haco.

'Maybe it is,' said the policeman, placidly. There's some people born green, and they remain green all their days; but that's not Sandy.'

'No; I'll never sit down under it,' said Sandy. 'I'm going to Buccleuch Place this time, Spens—to a better house and a better room, though it's high up at the roof.'

'Buccleuch Place! Why, don't you know that's where the Edinburgh Reviewers cultivated literature on a little oatmeal? I shouldn't wonder if you got their room.'

'Who were they?' asked Sandy.

'Smith, Brougham, and a lot of others.'

'Did they practise at the Infirmary?'

'No.'

'Oh, well, Robert, come along with my box. We haven't very far to go. I'm paying two shillings a week more, but I calculate I'll save it in 'buses and nearness to my work. Besides, I'm getting more for my teaching this year.'

'I'll give you a hand now, Sandy; you're panting violently. Come along with your old meal chest.'

Haco took it for half-a-dozen yards, then dropped the end on the pavement. 'Cabby!' he

shouted to a passing cabman. The cab stopped.
He asked the policeman to lift the box on to
the top and get inside; but Sandy vehemently
protested, and ordered the man to drive on.

'What! spend a shilling on a cab? That'll not
do for me.'

'Better that than burst a blood-vessel,' said
Haco, who felt his hands sore with the exertion
and his head swimming.

'I'll risk it,' said Sandy, panting, as they turned
into the broad square.

At the top of a long stair they found his room
waiting for him. It was double the size of the
one he had before. There was a carpet in it;
some portraits on the walls; two wide windows.

'Sandy, you're becoming a swell,' said Haco,
as he looked round about him.

'Here's to you, then,' said the policeman, with
a tumbler of ale in his hand.

CHAPTER V

EXPOSTULATIONS

SANDY BAXTER began the practice of his profession
to some extent as soon as he took a room in
Buccleuch Place. There was a student of the
Royal College of Surgeons who lived below him
who expected to become a full-fledged Royal
Collegian at the end of the year. Naturally, he
knew a great deal more than Sandy, having been
a good student, who was advancing to his double
qualification with honour. He practised a great
deal in a place called Potter's Row, and in the

Canongate and the Cowgate. He was already so popular that he had more cases on his hand than he could well undertake. Sandy's offer of occasional assistance was very acceptable to him. Not that Sandy had a great deal of time to bestow. He had still a large quantity of teaching on hand, out of which he paid his bills and fees ; and he was anxious, seeing that for this summer session he was a matriculated student of the University, to stand well either in botany or zoology, just to show the University fellows that an extra-mural man had as good stuff as they. He had a devouring anxiety, however, to excel in his profession, and he thought he could not begin too soon to understand sickness in its favourite haunts, to note disease before it came to hospital at all, and to see death where it overtook men amidst poverty and privation. He went down, therefore, with his friend to a Canongate close one evening, to see a case of consumption in its last stage.

'We can't do anything for her, you know,' said his friend. 'She's dying rapidly; but you'll be able to see how death looks in these cases.'

As they went through the close, Sandy stopped at a window emblazoned with the words, 'Roger Thorburn, LL.D., M.D.' He looked in at the door, and saw the seedy student who had been at the operating-table when Spens administered the chloroform. He called his friend's attention to him, and passed on. At the far end of the close they toiled up a ricketty wooden stair, from which much of the wood had been lifted to light fires. Once or twice Sandy's left leg went through the staircase as he ascended, and his friend explained to him pleasantly that there was extensive practice in sprained ankles and twisted thighs in these closes.

Nothing could be more miserable than the aspect of the room to which the students went. There was no fire in it; there was no furniture; the bed seemed to be made of the planks lifted from the

staircase. The woman who reclined on it was a
mere shadow of humanity, breathing out her life,
as it seemed, into a foul corrupted air, for the room
contained about a dozen of women, arms akimbo,
waiting to see her die.

Sandy's friend, assuming the air of an experienced physician, at once cleared the room
of half of them.

'You're only making it more difficult for her,'
he said, 'standing round here; and it's nothing
but curiosity to see her. Out you go, now! Out
you go! You can sit on the stairs if you like.
There's a fine draught blowing in at the second
window down, and, if it's risky for coughs, it's
better than the air of this room. Out you go!—
more of you. You can't all be near relations,
and she hasn't more than half-an-hour to live.
She's quite unconscious. In half-an-hour it will be
all over.'

'Sure, doctor, dear, it's see her doi we would like

to, now, the poor darlin', and put the salt on her breast, and loight the candles, and lay her out in a dacent way.'

'If you had spent the wake-money on her sooner, she needn't have been where she is,' said the collegian, shoving his way through the group, which declined to be pushed out of the room, and putting his hand upon the woman's pulse. 'Baxter,' he cried to Sandy, who, in the room of death, felt a strong inclination to whisper and to look sympathetic, whereas his friend rather increased the sound of his voice, and behaved altogether as if death were the normal condition of human beings, which was to be taken as a matter of course, without regret or emotion. 'Baxter, feel this. You have a finer nerve than I, if you can make anything out. I'll give her twenty minutes. Nothing can be done for her.'

Before she died the room filled up again, and wailing commenced, until a lane was made for a burly little man, bearing a book and a crucifix. As he came in, the collegian said,

'Now we may go. That's the priest. It is his turn. I'm sorry I had nothing better to show you than that, Baxter. It's a very common case, indeed. You will be none the worse, however, of knowing the final symptoms.'

'I think I will go in here for a little,' said Sandy, as they passed out of the close ; and he bade the collegian Good-night at Roger's door.

He had no previous intention of going in, for Roger was nothing to him except a student with a rather low reputation, whom he would have made it his duty to avoid. But he saw Haco Spens waiting at the counter, and he thought he might as well have a look at Roger's shop in Haco's company. As he lifted the latch and went in, the head of Roger, adorned with a gay smoking-cap, presented itself at the surgery door. The adviser did not at first recognise Sandy. In showing Spens into his own room, he came forward to the counter, and asked, with a bland voice,

'Is there anything I can do for you, sir?'

'You have a short memory for faces,' replied Sandy, 'for it isn't a year yet since I saw you in the waiting-room of the hospital. I came in just now because I saw Spens. With your leave, I'll follow him into your surgery.'

Haco was vastly amazed to see Sandy in Roger's surgery. He could not understand it, and he did not like it; it looked at first as if Sandy were following him about.

'I caught a glimpse of you,' exclaimed Sandy, 'as I was coming out from a case with another fellow. He's rather a swell in his way—Hodson, from Peebles. Did you ever meet him? He was *locum tenens* for a fortnight to one of the Peebles' doctors, and ran half over the county doing all kinds of practice.'

'Before he had his degree?' interpolated Roger, with much severity.

'He won't be M.R.C.S. till the end of autumn.'

'M.R.C.S.!' sniffed Roger. 'It's a degree that no self-respecting man would acknowledge. They give their double qualifications away, sir. They positively put them in an envelope and give them away.'

'It's my father's degree,' said Haco.

'Yes, but he belongs to the old school,' explained Roger, 'when the period of apprenticeship was only coming to a close, and the stricter days hadn't arrived. But I approve of their being strict. It keeps the profession select—it shuts the door upon the quacks. But, upon my word, till they begin to make it compulsory upon every medical man to have an M.D. degree, I believe we will not have gentlemen in every open berth.'

Roger spoke with the rapid ease of a physician of long standing, with a select practice among the nobility and gentry, whose expensive diseases remunerated him royally. Sandy and Haco were both a little taken in by his manner, and it was with a little accent of timidity that the former said,

'And you've graduated, then?'

'Graduated and double graduated,' said Roger. 'I am not only M.D., I am also LL.D.—a degree that gentlemen of our profession don't always earn. It requires a man to have, as I have, devoted double the usual time to his course, and then to graduate abroad.'

'Oh, you're a foreign graduate!' said Sandy, with some diminution of respect. 'Not American?'

'No, thank you.'

'Not Vienna?'

'Vienna! No. But let us pass off the topic. My degrees are on the wall, for the inspection of the world—both of them on rollers on the wall. I believe, however, that I have something to say

to you that you don't want this gentleman to
hear, Mr Spens. We will go to the outer surgery,
if you please, for a minute.'

'No occasion,' said Haco. 'Sandy Baxter knows
all about it He's quite as sorry as you, Dr Thorburn, for the cause of it.'

'You mean that death in the waiting-room,'
asked Sandy, 'and the payments Spens has been
making ever since? I think the whole thing is a
beastly imposition.'

The adviser turned his eye cruelly upon Sandy
and said nothing for a minute; then he remarked
slowly,

'Yes, I think it is rather a tax.'

'I've just come in from a death, and, upon my
honour, the symptoms weren't the least like those
I remember in the waiting-room.'

'A death! Where?'

'At the head of the close.'

'Confound your impertinence!' said Roger,

angrily. 'You are not out of your first year, and you come here, taking practice from a graduate. That was my case, I tell you; and it was nothing short of an impertinence—if it wasn't even a crime —for you to take it up.'

'It was Hodson's; it wasn't mine. And I am very certain there was no fee going, for there was nothing in the room but mere tumble-down sticks and a mattress.'

Roger cooled down a little as he perceived that Baxter had come in of his own accord, without being a companion, on the occasion, of Spens.

'Fee! no; I should think not. Who ever heard of medical students taking a fee?'

'Nobody,' said Sandy.

'Well,' said Haco, getting a little tired of Roger and his dingy surgery, 'there are some arrears, Thorburn. I think it comes to six pounds what I owe you.'

'Don't say you owe it to me,' said Roger, sharply.

'Six pounds!' murmured Sandy.

'All right. You know well enough what I mean. You are the fellow who pays the money, and who interests yourself in the poor man's family, and all that. Here you are!'

'If you take my advice, Spens,' said Sandy, looking at the transfer of notes, 'you'll make that payment the last you offer to him—the very last. What you ought to do about it, is to go to a lawyer. Who is this widow, Dr Thorburn? Where does she live? How many children has she? Was she ever as well off before as she is now? And where was this dead man buried? and who saw him buried? and'——

'That's a mouthful,' said the adviser, sarcastically. 'Have you arranged the meeting, Mr Spens? Am I cross-questioned at your instigation by this rather raw youth?'

'No, no,' said Haco. 'It's only Sandy's dogmatic way. He pitches himself into everything like that,'

'And are these payments to go on for ever,' continued Sandy. 'Two pounds a-week for ever—never to stop as long as Spens lives ?—week after week two pounds—two pounds—all because a fellow came into the hospital and, apparently died under the towel ! I'm not so very certain that he did die. I saw a fellow very like him one night doing the spring-heel business under a lamp-post. He seemed to me the living image of the man on the table. I don't say there was jookery-pookery, but I do say it looks to me very like as if there was.'

Roger opened a drawer, and, after rummaging a little, he drew out a signed certificate of death and handed it to Haco.

'Have you seen that ?' he asked.

Haco looked at the paper, and, shuddering, dropped it.

'No, and I don't want to see it. Mind your own business, Sandy. This is a matter between me and Thorburn. It's no use putting these questions.'

Sandy picked up the death certificate and read it.

'I can't make out the name,' he persisted.

'Is it of the least consequence whether you can or not?' asked Roger.

'What is his name?'

'Sandy, mind your own business.'

'Spens, you are hanging a millstone round your neck, and it will drag you under.'

CHAPTER VI

BOTANIZING

HACO and Sandy saw each other every morning now. The latter, on his way down to the Botanical Gardens, called at Haco's, and, sometimes, helped him to get out of bed, by the assistance of a tumbler of cold water unceremoniously douched from his wash-hand-stand to his pillow.

'Get up, you lazy beggar!' Sandy would say, when, with three or four hours' sleep to his own account, he would come into Queen Street and

find Haco not yet dressed, after a sufficient night's
rest.

Haco was no longer troubled with the appearance of the class-skeleton in his dreams, because,
though he had an announcement telling him that
'a subject' was at his disposal on the dissecting-
room table, he thought he could not possibly work
in a dissecting-room in summer, and decided not
to do it. He had anticipated attendance at Botany
and Zoology with enthusiasm. He was to give
Sandy a heat for at least one of the two medals.
It was a pleasure to him to think that Sandy
would not snatch at them with the same ease as
he had showed at the extra-mural, though he
would not grudge him success, if it came to him.

'Get up, you lazy beggar!'

That had been Sandy's greeting once and again,
as he showed himself at Haco's bedroom door; and
the pair had gone down the hill to the lecture-

room in the Botanical Gardens, thereafter, with different degrees of enthusiasm.

Sandy did not care two farthings for all the flowers in the world. He thought, on the whole, that when they were dried and hung up in bunches in the museum they looked very well. But a primrose on a river's brim, was simply a primrose to him, as was a moss rose, or a lily, or a pansy, or a dahlia, or a tulip. Sandy perceived, however, that a botanical knowledge was necessary to his becoming a skilled member of the profession to which he aspired ; so, without greatly caring about them, he took up flowers with dogged enthusiasm, and in a week knew infinitely more about them than Haco, who loved them and saw in them thoughts too deep for tears.

It was a misfortune for his knowledge that Haco should see anything in a flower beyond the distinguishing marks by which he could refer it to a given species or genus. He saw in it, however,

form and colour, which had an independent delight
of their own, apart from knowledge. It may have
been something in them which appealed merely to
the eyewash which lay at the back of his pupils,
whereas Sandy's view of them may have been the
view which touched the deeper centres of the
brain. Anyhow, the student who had the greater
joy in flowers was soon distanced in his knowledge
of them by the student who had the lesser, and
who, until the exigencies of his profession had
induced him to join the botany class, had never
given them a thought. To Sandy the vast models
in wood and wax, the glaring prints on the wall,
the uncouth phraseology of the classifications,
were an ever-renewed delight. To Haco they
brought nothing but bitterness and disappointment.
Knowledge, he thought, robbed the flowers of
their beauty, especially this awful bibliography,
dividing and subdividing, getting at every juice
and cell and atom, and calling the familiar loveli-

ness of the field and the garden by names which seemed to have tumbled down the centuries from schoolmen cradled among parchment. The result was that, while Sandy, sitting next Haco, had his note-book crammed with scientific observations, Haco had his pages covered with little sketches of leaves, and twigs, and wreaths, and petals. The further result was that, the Botanic Gardens being a place of enchantment in early summer, the day after the first cards had been called, Haco left Sandy's side and went out among the branch-shadowed walks, and finding a pond, with water-lilies pushing their way to the surface, he lay on a green knoll at the back of it, and watched the morning smoke of Edinburgh rising to the sky, in a blue vista through the trees. Then, when he got tired of that, he sauntered round to a palm-house, where the air was tropical, and, sitting at the foot of the columnar stems of the palms, he constructed a legend of the Indies, which was very pretty and enchanting as long as it lasted, but which did not help him to know the essential difference between *Elais* and *Rumex*.

Sandy burst in upon him after lecture, as he sat among the palms, and asked him anxiously if he were ill, that he had not been present that morning.

' No, not exactly ill; but awfully tired of " Vascular Tissue," Sandy. He makes me hate the whole vegetable kingdom, that man. Formerly, I used to sit down beside a bed of flowers and see nothing but elves and fairies pirouetting among them. Now that " Tissue " puts them under the microscope, the elves have vanished, the fairies have taken wing. I begin to regard them as enemies of my eye.'

' Spens, how will you ever be able to dispense drugs if you don't know what the drugs are made of ? This is fearful bosh you are talking. You are just playing truant because you are lazy, and shirking your work again. There is no pleasure in competing with a fellow like you. You'll have no chance of the medal if you go on like that.'

A further result was that, at the weekly examination, when the professor, handling his models, and, in his eagerness to impart and receive evidence of knowledge, losing count of the beginnings and ends of his words, asked Haco, as an intelligent-looking student, what he knew about a certain order of flowers. Haco knew nothing, while Sandy, promptly and vivaciously, told the professor everything the professor had told Sandy eight days earlier. At which the professor smiled, as if Sandy had discovered *hierochloë*. It was the same thing in the Natural History class. Sandy and Haco sat together as the professor arranged his buckies and his protoplasm, his birds' 'nebs' and his range of animal bones which resembled each other from the microscopic toe of a cheese mite to the telescopic bone in the rear of the pad of a foot of an elephant. He said they were all one, and Sandy, writing his notes as fast as he could, whispered to Haco,

' Flat Darwinism; I'm not going to be a monkey to oblige him.'

To which Haco replied,

' All one ? No, that's Spinoza, my dear fellow— Spinoza. He's over at the other shop—Logic, Metaphysics, &c. It's the biggest pot of the lot, Spinoza's. He boils them all down, protoplasm, bones, professors, and everything, into modes of the ultimate. Now, old " Bathybius," though they do say they mean to make a knight of him, is one of the most genial of the professorial modes I have listened to. I wish '—looking at his watch—' he were an ultimate at this moment.'

' Who is professor in this class, Mr Spens ?' asked ' Bathybius,' severely, having arrived half-way up from the mite's toe to the elephant's and being anxious to insert the human foot somewhere in the comparative scale, so as to demonstrate to the triflers in front of him that they were not so much better than a tom-cat, as they supposed themselves. Haco addressed himself to his notes at once, wishing 'Bathybius' was inside the Pantheist's pot, a restored and unconscious force, seeking for personality again in a world of consciousness; Haco's reading of Spinoza being that the all was for ever struggling into the infinitely little of life, so as to find mirrors in which ludicrously to see fragments of itself.

*　　*　　*　　*　　*

The first thing that reconciled Haco to his summer session was the organization of a botanical party. During the summer there were about a dozen of these parties, which went out hither and thither to collect the flora of half-a-dozen counties. The first excursion was to Arthur's Seat. It was in the evening, because the professor was obliged earlier in the day to be in the Cowgate to see that some young medical missionaries were keeping to their vows, and had had no intention of getting their education cheap or free for four years with the view of practising among the heathen, while they quietly walked into lucrative home practices in the fifth year of their studies. The professor joined them at a place called Samson's Ribs, while the moon shone white and free over the ramparts of Craigmillar and on the gray waters of Duddingstone. He gathered them in a group on the hard highway—there were two hundred of them—and looked on the wide, clear plain. There were two modern castles at their feet—modern, but still castles; and the professor, who was the most obliging man in the world, and who united archæology to his other pursuits, decribed them.

They were much in need of description, for from both castles a motley crowd emerged, who seemed to have been imbibing large draughts of ancient wine or something equally inebriating; and on the swards behind each castle moonlight dances commenced.

'Ah, they are very merry,' said the professor, 'though they are not so ancient as they look in the moonlight, and not so nautical as their name would seem to indicate—not the dancers; I mean the owners of the castles. Though, be it said to the honour of both castles, they employ nobody under two thousand a-year. It's a curious circumstance, and very honourable to them, that they give two thousand a-year to each man in charge of a department. I suppose they save on other things,' he added; 'for, though they published my "Cells, Great and Small," they did not remunerate me according to their reputation. Now, gentlemen all, this is the corner of Dunsappie Loch; we leave the open plain behind us, Duddingstone at our feet, and Duddingstone Village further along. Beautiful! beautiful! Showy in the extreme.

Now for the ascent. It's Saturday night, and we must remember the day that awaits us. It will be here—— What time is it ? Dear me! my watch has stopped. Mr Spens, is that you ? What time is it ?'

'Half-past eleven, sir.'

'Nonsense.'

'Yes, sir,' said half-a-dozen voices.

'Half-past eleven ! I couldn't have believed it. Now, gentlemen, in half-an-hour, if a vasculum is opened, or a spud inserted into the earth, I will apply to the *Senatus Academicus* to have that student expelled. I carry in my pocket at all times—to-day I have been in the Cowgate and used it freely—a book of sacred melodies. Mr Spens, I will trust to you telling me when twelve o'clock arrives, at which moment I will raise the tune, we will fall into line of march, and decorously go home to Edinburgh. In the meantime, we will have had a Pisgah-view of the city and the

Firth beyond. I regret—I greatly regret—that my engagements in the city have made it so late before I could reach you at Samson's Ribs, but we have time enough to collect all the characteristic flora before Sabbath morning arrives.

Haco had made a mistake of an hour in looking at his watch. The students at his back had affirmed his judgment, thinking he meant to be witty at the professor's expense.

When the professor led off again from Dunsappie to the top of Arthur's Seat, the wittier ones stayed behind, and sat down on stones, and lay on the dewy grass, and began to roar 'John Brown's Body.'

Sandy Baxter clung to the professor, helped him over dunes and ridges, asked him, with a deep, botanical air, whether he thought Hunter's Bog, through the continuous discharge of shots, would be likely to contain nitrogenous plants, and, altogether, was very pleasing with his inquiries.

'He's a sneak, that fellow,' said somebody, laying by his spud and vasculum. 'He knows that old "Tissue" always passes a man who attends his meetings. He gives a fellow who speaks through his nose fifty marks for his manner at a professional examination.'

'There you are quite wrong. Baxter is not a sneak at all. He is a very thorough and first-rate fellow, and sticks to the professor simply because he wants to get up botany.'

While the majority of the students went up Arthur's Seat, the minority stayed where they were, lit pipes, sang songs, threw stones into the black water of Dunsappie Loch, wished they had a glass of beer, and cried 'Hush!' as they listened to a mumbling voice come down to them explaining specimens as they happened to be found and presented by students.

At last, leap-frog, chaff, pipes, and loitering became unbearable; somebody said he heard 'Tissue'

making preparations for his meeting, whereupon
there was a stampede in the direction of Duddingstone.

'We have plenty of time yet,' said a student.
'The inns are open; let's go down and have some
fun. There's one of the nicest inns in the world
down there, with an open garden and unrivalled
beer. Who says?'

'I do!' 'I do!' 'So do I!' 'Hang "Tissue!"'
'The inn!' 'Duddingstone!' 'Hurrah! hurrah!'
'John Brown's body lies mouldering in the grave!'
'Hip, hip!' And the remainder of the students
who did not choose to go to the top of the hill,
the botany and the meeting, rushed to the grassy
ridge above Duddingstone Loch, tumbled down
with shouts, sped along the road past the old
gate and the pillory, and round a corner into an
inn. The songs that they sung were numerous
and merry, but they gathered no flowers and
they learnt no botany, and they missed hearing

the professor raise the tune.   Perhaps, when Haco
stood in the old pillory hours later, he really deserved to be there.   As they sang their way round
Samson's Ribs, they noticed that even the castles
were shut up.   There was nothing between Craigmillar and them but the moaning of the wind and
the light of the white moon on the plain.

CHAPTER VII

BOTANIZING in the spirit in which Haco botanized was of no great use. Zoologizing followed suit. He did not wish disenchantment to overtake him in his relations with the flowers and the birds; and systematic inquiry seemed to substitute for the glamour of attractive ignorance a repulsive knowledge which really did disenchant. He told Sandy, therefore, one morning, while they went down to the Botanic Gardens, that he didn't think he would compete. He would attain the dry bones of knowledge sufficient to enable him to get his fifty per cent. of the hundred marks required for an ordinary pass degree; more than that he did not care for.

Sandy was very contemptuous towards him when he told him.

'I don't care, Sandy; I believe it's a pity to know too much. Do you think we were sent here to cram every nook of the brain with information? No; I believe some were sent to sit down here and wonder and sing about it.'

'Wonder and sing about it! Yes; I could understand a chap, if he were a Homer or a Milton, saying that. But a minor poet, Spens—what's the use of that? I wouldn't give a well-crammed student for him any day. He's of no use whatever, with his ignorant wonder, and his "Oh's" and "Ah's" and "Ye's" and "Thou's." The fact is, Spens, you're a lazy beggar, and you're trying to excuse yourself to yourself.'

'I may be a minor poet, Sandy,' said Haco, with a touch of melancholy.

'Well, I'm precious glad there's nothing of that sort the matter with me, at any rate,' replied Sandy, hugging his textbook and whistling.

'No; I don't think *you* are a minor poet.'

It may be that Sandy hit off the nature of Haco's restlessness by telling him he was a minor poet—restless because he wished to produce something immortal, and always found his rhymes limited by the incompetency of the nature which Nature had given him to make them better. At any rate, he was restless and solitary, and one Saturday, when he had no companion to accompany him, he went up out of Princes Street, along the broad Lothian Road, to Fountain Bridge. Why it is called Fountain Bridge no one knows. There is no fountain; but there is a canal basin, and beyond the basin a bridge, through which barges, laden with clean coals and dirty refuse, perpetually go and come. A little way up the canal there is a 'rubber works,' which keeps sending water at the boiling point into the motionless stream. Opposite the works an old man, with 'a cast' in his eye, lends out boats at a shilling an hour to all who may care to purchase a little sweet and moveable leisure of that kind.

Haco went out and in among the bargees, who loafed along the banks, smoking and wearing a villanous air of go-ashore recklessness. He wondered if, beyond Linlithgow and in the neighbourhood of Falkirk, there might not sometimes be perilous moments upon the canal —if the great deep beneath its weeds did not present to the bargee mind problems of risk and excitement unknown to him. Else how could these thick-jawed men, smelling of illegitimate tar, bear on their faces the expression, 'We have been afloat. We have been nigh to death.

We didn't care a fig about it. We have a right
to be jolly now.'

He asked a bargee if there were storms beyond
Linlithgow, and if navigation was considered
insecure at Falkirk. There was nothing impolite
in his enquiry. He presumed that the man was
acquainted with starboard and port, and all the
difficulties which these turns of a bark to right
or left presented to the judgment of the steerer.
But the bargee only opened his jaws and spat.
The old man with the 'cast' in his eye, however,
said that on the canal a man didn't need to know
the polar star from the light inside a turnip-
lantern. The less he thought of navigation the
better; let him look to his beasts. He also
volunteered the information that when a steam-
boat ran between the east and west he had
frequently seen passengers arrive in the last
stages of sea-sickness.

'All imagination!' said the old man, dismissing

the power of illusion as if it were a function of no moment whatever. 'Always look a-head when you come to a bridge,' he added, pushing Haco and his boat out with a hook. 'A bargee never stops.'

'Perhaps he's like the poor gentleman with the cork leg, who, when some of his esteemed relations came to beg, rudely assaulted them from behind. I forget whether the failing was the cause or the consequence of the cork leg. I will look it up when I go home. It was in Rotterdam, or Amsterdam. Derwick was the poor Dutchman's name. He now procures degrees—five pounds a-piece. Oh, you are not interested; then I'm off.'

The country behind Edinburgh, into which Haco rowed, rewarded him beyond his expectations. The canal became weeded and picturesque, and from the villas of Morningside and Merchiston picturesque figures in blue and white and gold held parasols to the sun as they sauntered on the banks. There was deeply-wooded Corstorphine on the left of him; there were the undulating Braid Hills and the ridge of the Pentlands on his right hand.

'The Castle of Merchiston!' said Haco, looking at the flag flying on its turrets. 'Somebody discovered logarithms there. Logarithms! And he has handed himself down to the infamy of every schoolboy. Why have men at all times been so inquisitive? Yes, it is better to be ignorant somewhat, and to wonder.'

He shot through bridge after bridge, and rapidly got away into the country, far beyond Slateford, and on the way to Linlithgow; for he never stopped to descend to the inns to drink bottled beer. Bottled beer had no attraction for him since that Saturday night at Duddingstone when he had swallowed some, and found next morning that he was nearly as ill as he had been with his first smoke. He had gone far into the country, when it occurred to him that he would tie up his boat and saunter a little. The butterflies

were on the wing, the bees were singing among
the yellow heads of the flowers, and all round
about him there was the subdued hum of an
invisible but active life of winged things. These
impressions of actual life in the warm air were
more to him than knowledge. He was glad he
had not a vasculum and a spud; glad that he
was among the quacking of ducks and the
husky cawing of crows, with heaven above and
the green carpet at his feet, for the fields ran
up to the edge of the canal where he was, and it
was all waving clover or plains of young corn. He
sauntered away from his boat, and presently lay
down to his favourite occupation of dreaming,
when by there came, a few minutes afterwards,
a soft footfall, which Haco thought was that of
a browsing animal. It was not, however; it was
a girl knitting, and when Haco put his hat off
his brow, rose on one elbow and looked, he saw
that it was Tibbie Baxter.

'My dear Tibbie, tell me,' he said, springing to his feet and rushing precipitately towards her, 'that my eyes don't deceive me. Is it really you?'

Tibbie, too, looked hard at him on the grass, but he lay so that she could not distinguish his face, though her poor heart gave a great throb at the resemblance to Haco.

She stopped knitting, and a blush gathered on her cheeks, which faded away into pallor while she held out her hand to him.

'Why, my dear Tibbie! This is—it's you know —how has it happened? Have you come over the Firth of Forth on a broomstick, you witch?'

'I am living with my uncle's people, over there,' said Tibbie, pointing a mile away to a homestead, shining in the sunlight, from which the pleasant sound of cart-wheels was borne to their ears.

'I didn't know you had an uncle in this part of the world, Tibbie.'

'Oh, yes, indeed, my mother's brother. He's a

large farmer. You were lying on his clover a little ago. My father packed me off here one day '——

And Tibbie faltered, and gave a side-glance at Haco, with much meaning.

'You don't mean that day you and I stood at the paling near Binkie, and—what was it again, that happened ? I forget.'

'You don't forget, Mr Haco. Nor do I, Mr Haco. My father was never angry with me before in his life—never.'

'I thought I made it all right with him, Tibbie. I promised him I would never kiss you again.'

'Did you ?' said Tibbie, with a faltering voice, in which the sound of disappointment seemed to reach Haco's ears.

'That is,' he added, beginning to sophisticate, and looking at Tibbie's glowing face with a responsive throbbing at his own heart—'that is—I —yes, I'm afraid I must say I gave him my word of honour that I wouldn't kiss you again.'

Tibbie's face blazed. She said Mr Haco and her father made very free with her in their conversation, and she wished that, for the future, they would let her be, without passing words of honour over her.

'Now you are offended, Tibbie.'

'No, I am not, Mr Haco. I am very glad to meet you, so well as you look. And how is Sandy, if you know?'

'I saw him yesterday morning. We go to the same classes this session, you know. Sandy is a wonderful fellow, you know. I thought he would have some difficulty about medals in botany; but not a bit of it. He'll be at the top there, just as he was at the extra-mural. It's an honour to know Sandy at college. At the weekly examinations, whenever "Tissue" has the least difficulty about getting an answer, it's always "Mr Baxter, Baxter, you know this sub-kingdom," and, sure enough, he does know.'

Tibbie looked a little proud of her kinship to
Sandy ; then she said,

'W—won't you be getting some medals, Mr
Haco?'

'If I do, it will be by a tremendous fluke,' he
answered, passing away from a subject which was
disagreeable to him.

Then they stopped and looked into the canal,
and for fully five minutes said nothing. He
gazed ardently at her, however, and she looked
ardently unconscious of his gaze.

'Tibbie,' he suddenly broke out, 'I can't stand
this. Did you ever play at coach-horses when
you were a little thing? This way—look. Stand
at my side. Give me that knitting stuff to put
in my pocket. Now, you pass your right hand
over and catch my hand, and my other intertwines ;
and, now, we run along the bank to the boat.
There's no harm in that, is there? Your father
couldn't say I broke my word then, could he?

I haven't attempted to kiss you, Tibbie, have I?
This is rather good fun, isn't it?'

Tibbie presently screamed with laughter as
they ran along the canal, their hands intertwined
at each other's back; and when they came to the
boat and looked into it, she was rather sorry than
otherwise to miss the pressure of his hand.

'I think when a fellow gives his word of honour
to a girl's father that he won't'——

'I can steer a boat,' said Tibbie, abruptly. 'If
you don't go up past my uncle's, but down towards
Edinburgh, I could sit and steer.'

'You really are a nice girl, Tibbie,' said Haco;
'you make such pleasant, sensible suggestions.
But you interrupted me. I think I am behaving
very well, don't you?'

'I think you are,' said Tibbie, still with that
accent of disappointment, conveying a sort of
latent intimation that she wished he would not
insist upon being such a very, very good boy.

For an hour-and-a-half he rowed her backward and forward within the circuit of half-a-mile. Then she said she would have to go back because the cattle were beginning to low in the fields. They stood under a bridge just before they bade each other Good-bye.

'I don't think there is any harm in saying Good-bye as if we were a brother and sister, Tibbie.'

Tibbie thought there wasn't any harm, and their lips met under the bridge.

CHAPTER VIII

A NEW CLASS

SANDY BAXTER was becoming popular. It was known of him at the houses where he supervised the Latin exercises and the Greek pothooks of boys attending the Institution, the Academy, and the High School, that at the extra-mural he had won all the medals. It was not so well-known that the attendance at the extra-mural was limited to Sandy, or that Sandy had been his own competitor. Not that Sandy deserved any less credit on that account; for his marks were so high that the probability is not three lads out of three hundred, had they been competing with him, would have achieved similar distinction. The popularity took rather an embarrassing form for Sandy. He taught for a couple of hours in a house outside the Grange Cemetery — an institution for the reception of the permanently silent, which lies in one of the newer suburbs of Edinburgh—and one evening, as he was putting himself into his outer coat, the elder sister of the boys asked him if he would care to meet some people next Friday night. With perfect alacrity Sandy said he would; but the evening had not been too happy for him. The people were extremely nice, seventeen girls being all that could be desired by the eye of the susceptible youth, and the five other young men than Sandy, who were expected to dance with them, being not too objectionable. Sandy, however, could not dance. His father had never allowed him to learn, notwithstanding the protests of Mrs Baxter. It was his disagreeable duty, therefore, that evening, to sit in a corner by himself, hopelessly given up by the elder sister of his pupils, and coldly scanned by the dozen damsels who were waiting their turn to be whirled.

'Oh, do you not dance?' said the elder sister's mother.

'Are you above this sort of thing?' asked the mother's husband.

'Mr Baxter,' remarked one of the boys who would have greatly liked to dance, but who could find no partner except his aunt, who was fifty, 'rise up and show them the way.'

But Sandy would not move. Privately, he had some of his father's contempt for the bobbing and ducking, and twirling and turning. He thought human beings might be otherwise advantageously engaged; yet he suffered so much from his incompetence on that occasion, and again at a house in Morningside, when, being asked to dance, he

stood up and chanced it, feeling that he had
observed enough at his last party to entitle him
to try, that he determined to learn. His first
efforts were all by himself in his high room at
Buccleuch Place.

When he came in from his work he would change
his coat and imagine a companion, and dance round
his own table with her till he was giddy. That did
not teach him much, however. He did rather
better with a broomstick, which his landlady happened to leave about. He danced with the broomstick, hitting his bedroom door with it, knocking
the fender with it, whacking the table, indenting
his cupboard, and thudding the floor till he became
aware that he was being scrutinized through the
keyhole, whereupon he stopped and rang his bell
for some more cold water.

'Dear, dear,' said his landlady, 'I was looking
for that broomstick and couldn't find it. It was
careless to leave the broomstick in your room.'

And she took it away.

After his practice by himself, Sandy, with confidence in himself, essayed to dance at Morningside. He thought a waltz was the easier of two dances of which he had the option, the secret of it being a determination to get round the room at a great rate, without bumping or tumbling. By a little dash and courage, he had no doubt he could manage it very well; but he was surprised to find that between the sounds of the piano and the movement of the feet there seemed to be a connection. He had not thought of that, never taking the least interest in musical sound of any sort; when he dashed off, therefore, with his partner, it was exactly as if he had had the broomstick. He hit the pianist on the back with her, he threw her against other dancers, he tumbled her over the fender, and drove her against the lintels of the door, until, to save herself from fainting, the poor girl was obliged to halt and say,

'If you please, Mr Baxter, we will sit down now.'

Sandy saw, after that, that he must get some little insight into this mysterious double movement of the feet. He must make it, like zoology and chemistry, a matter of knowledge, acquire it, and afterwards practice it as he meant to do his profession. For, oddly enough, at these gyrations, he found his position as a medallist of very little use to him. Nobody seemed to care for latent distinction of that sort. Could he dance well? Then he was popular. Was he a bad dancer? Then he was unpopular.

'I may require to dance when I am entering a practice,' he reflected. 'I will learn forthwith.' Exactly as he went at his studies—that is, with all his heart and soul—Sandy determined to go to his dancing. He had seen a board on the side of a house in Nicolson Square, not far from the University, intimating that, three storeys up, there was a 'Dancing Academy.' He made an elaborate calculation whether an hour at this academy would rob him of any advantages at his classes. 'Let him see'—counting the hours, and the engagements in each of them, with the fore-finger of his right hand upon the fingers of his left. 'Let him see: there was Botany in the morning; Zoology in the forenoon; Anatomy in the afternoon; an hour's teaching between Botany and Zoology; an hour's teaching between Zoology and Anatomy; three hours' teaching afterwards, and his work to prepare for next day. Could he do it? Yes, he could. Therefore he would do it.'

Accordingly, he went into Nicolson Square one evening, ascended three storeys, and scrutinized a brass plate, on which 'Dancing Academy' was repeated. He knocked, and had the door opened to him by a curious individual, whom he seemed to have seen before. He was shown into a hall, which consisted of the greater portion of the flat, gutted and enlarged to one room. There was a little raised dais at one end, a couple of fiddle-cases reclined in a corner, and a brazen instrument, with masterly potentialities of wind in its inside, shone from a wall. There was no other furniture or decoration, and, except the individual who admitted him, neither master nor pupil present.

'I want to learn to dance,' said Sandy, looking inquiringly at the strange figure he seemed to have seen before.

'Yes, I suppose so.'

'Are you the teacher?'

'I'm the master of ceremonies.'

Sandy thought he had a heavy flavour of spirits about him which he would have been better without.

'What's that?' he asked.

'I've been master—master of the ceremonies,' he replied, with a slight hiccup, which he suppressed, 'to Hengler, sir; to Sanger, sir; to Orde—greater than any of 'em.' (Hiccup.) 'Orde, sir, was a man

who understood genius and sympathized with it.
Now, look at this.'

And the master of the ceremonies, to demonstrate
his possession of genius, severed himself from himself, threw his head away and caught it, as if his
trunk were a cup and his head a ball, made a
rotatory movement with his right leg, as if he
were a grindstone in full employment, and nipped
himself in two.

Sandy was lost in amazement. He had never
been to a circus, or a theatre, or a penny gaff. But
he saw that this was a phenomenon which contra-
dicted all his anatomical knowledge. He proceeded
to logically demonstrate to the phenomenon that
he really could not physically do what he was
doing.

'You perceive,' said Sandy, 'that the cervical
vertebræ are so set upon the neck, and depend so
consistently upon the lumbars on the one hand,
and the skull on the other, that a person who

threw his head off his neck would die. That is
how men are hanged.'

'Is it?' said the master of the ceremonies. 'And
how do you know I ain't been 'anged. I never
said I wasn't. Did you never hear of a 'anged
man comin' alive again? Lor' bless you, them
doctors know nothing. I had a pal at Orde's for
years who had swung for it at—I won't say
where—and I'm the only contortionist now; but
he was the onliest before he got planted. His
neck was broken before ever he came to be
hung up. It didn't matter to him, Calcraft
breakin' it again. Not a bit. Mr Calcraft, when
he cut him down, he reconnized him as the Great
Snake, an' he bundles a bag o' sawdust in the
quicklime hole in the gaol corner, an' lets him
out. Says Calcraft, "I'm paid for a-hanging of
ye. I ain't paid for a-murderin' of ye, Snake, my
friend. I broke your neck for the law once—once
is enough. I don't entertain no mean enmity

to ye. You come along o' me. I shouldn't wonder
if you'd be a job to me afore long." He was a good
sort, was Calcraft. But that Snake's gone, and I'm
the only Snake left. I wish I wasn't so fond o'
the bottle, though. It keeps me from the higher
walks. Says my medical attendant to me, " Snake
if you was to take my advice, you would leave
the bottle alone, and the Emperor o' the French
and all the crowned heads they would take you
up—they would, indeed. They would take ye
up to amuse their young 'uns. You might have
the run o' the Tooleries, Snake," says my medical
attendant. And I feel I'm debarred from the higher
walks'—putting his hand into the inside of his
jacket, craning his neck towards a bottle, with a
movement like a disreputable swan, extracting the
cork with his teeth, and absorbing some spirits.

' What do ye do it for, then ?' asked Sandy, who
had no temptation to do anything off the even

path of rectitude, which lay as straight before him as a coach road.

'Because·I'm wicked, and was born wicked, and don't like to be nuffin else. I've been ruined though. I'm a master of ceremonies; and here's proprietor a-coming', and don't you say I carry the drink about wi' me. It's an improvement on the liquorice stick and tamarind water.'

'If you don't betray yourself, it's none of my business,' said Sandy, turning from the contortionist to a little old man with a stooping figure, accompanied by a pair of bouncing daughters, who looked contemptuously at the Snake and affectionately at Sandy. One of them, a head and shoulders taller than Sandy, with a countenance of the most frank and open description, asked him if he had come to dance.

'Yes; to learn.'

'Have you ever danced before?'

'No.'

'How nice!' said the other daughter. 'Father, here is a gentleman come to learn who has never danced before.'

The little old man went to the corner for his fiddle, took it out, screwed it, resined it, scraped it till it screamed, and came forward to the middle of the floor, his body swaying with a rhythmic motion and his head nodding, as he kept drawing his bow across the strings.

'To be a dancer,' he said, looking critically at Sandy, 'one thing is needful—a pair of legs.'

'I've got that,' said Sandy.

'With a pair of legs,' he continued, 'be they thick or thin, hard or soft, short or long, I can make a dancer. But that is not enough. I want good dancing, and that requires a good pair of legs, which have firmness in the brawn and suppleness at the joints. Added to which, sir,' he said emphatically, striking the Snake over the head with his bow when he showed an irresistible

tendency to turn himself into a grindstone, 'I
want music in a man's soul, for this dancing is
first cousin to sound. As so'—and he played
with extreme rapidity, some notes of a reel, to
which his daughters instantly responded by shoot-
ing out their elbows and bobbing as if they were
marionettes pulled by wires—'as so; you observe
my daughters. And I want a guinea a quarter,
payable on the spot, for the inestimable privilege
of my teaching.'

'A guinea is a large sum of money,' said Sandy.

He looked at the Snake for justification of the
extravagant magnitude of the sum. But that
worthy was craning his head in the direction of
his inside pocket.

'I thought,' pursued Sandy, 'I could learn to
dance on less than a guinea. I'm afraid I'll have
to give it up altogether if I have to pay as much
as that.'

The tall daughter now threw up her arm, told

her father to retire to his daïs, asked the master
of the ceremonies what he was about, called out
in a commanding voice, ' *Valse à trois temps,*' and
before Sandy knew what he was about, he was
circling like a mill-wheel, while his tall partner
looked down at him graciously. He tripped and
stumbled and almost fell, but the Amazonian
strength of his partner kept him up, and he went
six times round the hall without stopping.

' That isn't dancing, you understand,' said the
partner, as the screaming of the fiddle came to an
end and she stood with Sandy's arm round her
waist, under the brazen instrument. ' Snake,' she
continued, disengaging herself—' Snake, you will
do the same dance with my sister. Now, keep
your eyes on Snake's feet, sir, and you will
notice the difference.'

' *Valse à trois temps!*' exclaimed the well-look-
looking Amazon; the fiddle began to scream, the
Snake wove his arm about the sister, and Sandy

perceived, what he had never noticed before, that
this dancing was an art, not to be practised with
the impunity of ignorance, but to be seriously
learnt, with as much care as he bestowed upon his
sciences. While he waltzed, the Snake, who had
seemed so repulsive to Sandy, craning at his bottle
and making his criminal brag, became animated
and inspired. His partner and he went round,
borne up by sound, as it appeared, and Sandy determined to get some of that aerial grace for his
money, if he could. He told the master that, after
all, he thought a guinea not so very much, and
before leaving he paid his money, saying he would
return again at the same hour till he learnt how to
dance.

'You are fortunate,' said the fiddler, 'in having
the floor to yourself. Our large classes begin as
your hour comes to an end.'

'It's not the first time I have been so fortunate,'
murmured Sandy, going down into Nicolson Square.

CHAPTER IX

EARLY MORNING

LADY MARY HAY continued her work in the wards, and Haco went on assisting her. She liked to have the lad in her train, for, though the students came in their little crowds to hear Crum expatiate on cases, and at the bedsides put his comments into their note-books, they were all rather in her than in his following. Spens was the power behind the throne, however. It was admitted that though Lady Mary was tolerant to everybody who approached her, and even sweet

and obliging in her manner, with Spens only was
she friendly. It was universally affirmed in the
hospital that she was in love with him, and that
the baronet's son and the earl's sister were likely
to make a match of it.

Mrs Blake was the author of the rumour, and
it took its rise in this way. One of Lady Mary's
little boys had an excision of the knee joint performed on him. For some reason or other, he was
shifted from her ward to a neighbouring one,
in which there were none but patients who had
long reached their maturity. Dr Crum expected
that the boy would be noisy and restless all night,
and that he would, probably, interfere with the
sleep of children as much in need of rest as
himself. Lady Mary parted with him with great
reluctance. She could not follow him into the
men's ward, greatly as she would have liked to
do it. She got Haco, however, to arrange with

the dressers in the men's ward that he should be
allowed to take the night watch.

The night watch in the hospital was new to
Haco. He had never passed a midnight among
the sufferers, and on this occasion his experience
of it left an indelible impression of misery on
his mind. What a responsibility it was! On one
bed lay an old man, destined on the morrow for
the surgeon's table. He could not sleep, and while
the town bells were tolling an hour after midnight
he rose uneasily, and with slow, painful movements took himself out to the cold corridors and
stood in one of the windows, thinking of the
white mutch of his wife, whom he had left in
a sea-dell upon a northern slope of Scotland, and
wondering whether to-morrow were to bring to
him the end of all or the beginning of a new
period of painless life.

The ward was high, and the sounds went up as
if into the arch of a cathedral—not sounds of

harmonious praise, but the bitter groans of the
agonized and dying. All through the midnight
the little boy whimpered, and asked Haco to put
his hand upon the plaster cast under which his
excised limb reposed. 'He felt it falling to pieces,'
he said. 'He was bleeding to death,' he murmured; and Haco, fearing hemorrhage and his
own inability to stop it, kept rising from the
surgical table and walking from the fireplace to
the boy's bedside, not sure whether he should
call the nurse and awaken the house-surgeon, or
act upon his own scared judgment. He went out
into the corridor and saw the poor patient shivering
in a window.

'You would be better in bed, my dear fellow,'
he said. 'Take a hold of my arm and get back
to your place.'

'I canna help wanderin'. But let me alone,'
was the reply; and Haco returned to the boy's
bedside.

Hour after hour passed; the groans from some of the beds ceased, and it was apparent that sleep had descended to the relief of some of them. One sufferer, however, who had been wrestling through the livelong night, raised himself on his elbow opposite Haco, and, as if electrified, leaned glaring at him. He made no motion. He simply kept his glassy eyes fixed upon Haco. He had ceased breathing.

'Do you want anything?' Haco called out, beginning to feel a cold shiver in his back.

The man's jaw fell, and it was apparent that the spirit had gone.

'He's awa',' said the voice of a sleepless patient, who had been watching the fight of death from an opposite bed. 'That's the third this week. It makes a body shiver. They put up a screen when a man dees—that screen at the back o' the ward door. Shut his een and put up the screen.'

Haco did as he was told, in obedience to the

voice of experience which dictated to him.   He
saw from the blue light at the blinds that midnight
had given way to morning, and as it streamed in
upon the ward, he raised a corner and looked out.

The tragedy of death was at his elbow : he had
not yet recovered the shock of that arresting gaze,
when he heard a voice from a bed querulously
demanding a Bible.

'My Bible! Where's my Bible ? I cannot do
without my Bible.'

It was now broad daylight.   Haco turned and
offered his assistance in finding the missing book.
It was a leather-covered school Bible and lay out
of sight beneath the devotee's pillow.

'Here you are,' said Haco, finding it for him.

'That has been my razor-strop for ten years,
sir,' said the patient, beginning to whet his blade
on the cover and putting the volume away without
reading after it had got a satisfactory edge.

It was a relief to Haco to find that tragedy

and comedy existed under the same roof, and that even death could not eliminate some of the latter.

As morning became more assured, Haco knew that the outer gates of the hospital had been opened, and that traffic was commencing in the streets. He did not at once know, however, when there was the sound of carriage wheels at the gate, that Lady Mary had come early to hear of her little charge.

She came straight to the ward door, and her face wore a bright, fresh expression as she stood looking in, so making sure that her presence could embarrass nobody.

'I may, I suppose?' she said, softly, holding out her hand to Haco, who advanced to meet her. 'You have not had any help all night, have you? You have had a good night's work. Ah! the screen!'

Together they stood at the bedside of the little boy. He had gone to sleep, and was evidently dreaming of nice things, for he smiled peacefully.

'We will not disturb him,' said Lady Mary, going out into the corridors. 'He is going to live, poor boy! Dr Crum never loses a life, hardly.'

They stood in the window looking down on the hospital gardens, where only the sparrows were out as yet.

'You are looking so tired and done up,' she said, sympathetically. 'This night-work is very trying for you. I'm so much obliged to you; indeed, so deeply grateful to you for your help to my little patient. You know I consider him mine. I felt all through the night, when I wakened and thought of the boy, that he was in good hands. Any ordinary dresser would not have given me that confidence, Haco.'

'My dear Lady Mary, to have earned your gratitude is a great deal more to me than the little trouble it was to sit up through the night. The poor boy went on all night putting questions to me about you, till he fell asleep. He insisted that you had promised to come and see him early, and he never stopped asking if it was early yet.'

'You will now feel, Haco, that you are almost a member of the profession.'

Lady Mary looked anxiously at him as they stood in the recess. He answered her by passing his hand through his hair and sighing. He looked jaded. Lady Mary was sorry for his fatigue and his pale face, and was more tender in her manner towards him than she had ever allowed herself to be.

'It is well, Haco, that, like me, you are young and elastic. This night's work will not kill you.'

'No, indeed; I should be very poor stuff if it did. But I shall never be young again. I have seen a man die—for the second time, as you know.'

'Yes, the screen; I noticed it. Dr Crum told me he feared there would be a death in the ward during the night. But that must not age you, Haco.'

'I shall never be young again. Why, he leaned upon his elbow and looked at me, and his jaw fell, and he was gone. This moment wrestling for his life; that moment silent—silent as the tomb he is going to. Extinguished, as I might extinguish a rushlight, with the breath of my lips, by blowing it out. You know who it is that says, "Nature's pluck is extinction." You heard him that crowded Sunday night at the Hopetoun Rooms, when he was demonstrating the origin of life—how physical it was. Well, the end is not like the beginning, yet I saw that man die, and I read extinction in his face—the ghastly horror of surprise in his jaw, that he had been snapped to nothingness so suddenly after all his hopes and expectations. I am aged; yes, I shall never be young again—never—never'——

'Dear Haco,' said Lady Mary, still in the recess, 'you take things too bitterly. You should confine yourself to your own sphere. It is yours, it is mine, to soothe the dying, to rescue, if we can, the endangered, to help pain and alleviate accident, and to leave these greater questions of the future life to other men and women. Let the Church answer these questions: Do I go to nothingness when I die? Is there a hereafter? You may rely on it, I think, that the Power which has produced life will be faithful to its idea, if it is a good one. It may be a blunder,'—Lady Mary sighed—'a wrong and a cruel idea, one which the Power had much better never have imagined. Well, what then? It is not for long—not if we live forty years beyond the Biblical span. What is a century to the geological record? What is a human life to the organizer of the solar system?'

'I shall never be young again,' murmured Haco, the dark rings blackening under his eyes. 'It is a revelation to me. I see it all—the whole play and its meaning. They talk of people aging into gray hairs in a night. My head is gray.'

'No, dear Haco, it is not gray. It is exactly the colour it was yesterday, when the sun shone in upon you bending over that poor little boy's bed; and I felt, as I looked at you, He might be a girl —he might be a younger sister.'

Haco looked at her and with an imploring glance, he said,

'I will repeat you something I have read since I came into the wards. I found it in the torn corner of a newspaper, where a reviewer had quoted it. It has refused to leave my recollection.

> ' " Ah, love let us be true
> To one another ! for the world, which seems
> To lie before us like a land of dreams,
> So various, so beautiful, so new,
> Hath really neither joy, nor love, nor light,
> Nor certitude, nor peace, nor help for pain ;
> And we are here, as on a darkling plain
> Swept with confused alarms of struggling and flight,
> Where ignorant armies clash by night." '

'No, it is not so bad as that,' said Lady Mary.

'Why,' continued Haco, 'in the very recess of this window where we are standing, a gra-

velled veteran stood for hours—all through the
midnight. To-morrow he will mount the table,
and will refuse to take chloroform, and Nature,
shocked at the heart, will pluck him. I asked
him, as he stood there moaning low to himself,
what he was thinking about. "My wife's white
mutch," he replied. He is a poor stone-polisher
from the north, and all that remains to him the
night before his death—for he will die; Crum
says a hundred to one that he will die—is the
recollection of his wife's white mutch. Lady Mary,
I believe that Nature's pluck is extinction, and
that nothing is left us but love—

> " ' Ah, love, let us be true
> To one another.' "

Lady Mary looked at him. He had been very
ardent and excited, and, though she had put love
by as not her mission in life, she felt a momentary
thrill as their eyes glanced and kindled on meeting
each other's confronting gaze.

'Notwithstanding your feeling about old age, you
are really very, very young yet, Haco. Do not
dream so much, and act more, and you will be less
sad. And now,' she added rapidly, 'you have taken
my hand, and you have had my fingers at your lips
exactly as if I were Youth at the helm and you were
Pleasure who had crept away from the prow; and
you will be going away with the impression that I
have allowed you to fall in love with me. I have
not, Haco; I have not indeed. All that is out of
the question for me. I am serving in this temple
of the weak and the sick and the dying, and must
be allowed to be a priestess without solicitation
of affection. I like you, Haco, and shall always
be pleased to help you in any other way than with
the love you seem to invite. Now, when I am
removed to Vienna, I shall always think of you
with gratitude for the assistance you have given
me in my work. But—no love!'

She turned and saw Mrs Blake at her back; but

she was perfectly serene and self-possessed—a circumstance which the head nurse attributed to her ancient descent, and not to her hypocrisy, to which she would have attributed it in the case of a girl with a common origin.

'I can assure you,' said Mrs Blake, 'though I came upon them in the corridor, and Mr Spens, at six o'clock in the morning, with his face unwashed, proposing marriage to her, and her saying, "No, love," she turned round on me as if nothing were occurring. See what it is, Mrs Pechey, to have a family tree.'

So spoke the head-nurse to another head-nurse who visited her in her room, and took something out of a bottle labled 'Poison.'

'A boy and a girl,' said Mrs Pechey.

'No doubt,' said Mrs Blake.

CHAPTER X

AIRING THE CHILDREN

THE summer session in Edinburgh can grow very monotonous. Half the professors are gone away to the country to enjoy themselves in the sunshine, and to write one new lecture against the coming session. One is enough, for the average duration of a professor's life is twenty-five years after his appointment, and twenty-five lectures in that time amply fulfil all the purposes of prelection. The remainder are written in the first year of occupancy of the chair, which demands unprecedented effort. It does nobody any harm—not even the students—if professors go on remembering for five-and-twenty years what a strain they had during the first six months, and sitting down under the burden of the recollection of it till they die of gout and whist. The other half, who remained in town, were at all times too busy to occupy themselves with the students after class hours.

The University provided no common basis of amusement for its lads. If Haco had not had his yacht brought over from Binkie and anchored in Granton Harbour, he would have been as ill off as his neighbours, many of whom, from sheer absence of resource, loitered about public-houses, billiard-rooms, and such-like places, day and night, till they ruined themselves, body and soul. There was, to be sure, an institution near his own rooms called 'The Philosophical,' where telegrams of all the important events of the day were to be seen, and where returned Indians, retired tradesmen,

clergymen, schoolmasters, and lawyers, moved
about among frames, reading. It was not un-
amusing to notice, as Haco did, that these men
held a parliament with themselves behind each
frame. According to the tone of each leader or
article they seemed to read, their lips moved and
their fists clenched, and they pshawed or slapped
their knees. Sometimes a returned Indian would
collar a clergyman from behind a frame where
there was a print warranted to give full reports
of divorce cases, and carry him off to a frame
where there was a misspelling in the name of a
village in the jungle of an unvisited corner of an
Indian Presidency, and pointing to the missing *h*
or the unnecessary *g*, would fulminate till everybody looked. The clergyman would then steal
back to his divorce case, and gobble the evidence
with an alacrity which was amazing to behold.
Or Haco would go into the book-room, and, from
a table, would lift off the last new book and pore

over it, on a sofa, till it was ten o'clock, and he was asked to go. With his yacht in Granton Bay, however, he did a great deal better than a great many students, though Sandy expostulated with him when he talked of bringing it over, had assured him that if it was once introduced on the Edinburgh side of the Firth there would be no more work done.

As for Sandy, the result of the first class-examinations soon settled his place. Haco had attended both, and done, as he thought, very well. When, however, he heard the results read out, first by ' Vascular Tissue' and then by ' Bathybius,' he understood, once for all, that Sandy was the better man.

' On the whole,' mumbled "Tissue," ' the papers are fair, average papers. But there is one student who shows to me that much better work might be done by the rank and file. Mr Baxter—Mr Alexander Baxter—I'm obliged to give him the

full value—one hundred per cent.—cent. per cent.!
The showy flower that I submitted for your
examination and description, Mr Baxter has
examined and described so that I cannot sub-
tract a single mark from him. On this occasion
only, I will confess to you—— Janitor! ('Yes,
sir!') Janitor! turn out the two benches at the
back of the class-room, and call cards after they
are removed. ('Yes, sir!') On this occasion——
Stop that noise, will you, janitor! ('Yes, sir!')
Remove two more benches. ('Yes, sir!') Now
that we are almost alone, I must say that, on the
whole, the papers have pleased me greatly—
greatly. One hundred per cent.! Mr Alexander
Baxter, if you are not standing on this platform,
some years hence, illuminating the minds of suc-
ceeding generations, then I am much mistaken.
So far as you have gone, taking the first six
weeks of you as a botanist, you are the most
accurate, the most perfectly, minutely informed

of any botanist I happen to know, or have known. Janitor! ('Yes, sir!') We will not call cards to-day.' ('Yes, sir!')

Haco, on the contrary, along with fifty others, only got about fifty-two per cent. on his Botany paper. In the Natural History class it was very much the same, much to the surprise of everybody, Sandy Baxter included; for it was observed on the examination day, that Sandy had shot through his paper sooner than anybody, and, with a slight air of disgust, had cast his leaves between the stuffed fore-paws of a fox, who surveyed the class-room, as if he were in despair of answering anything. But he had answered everything, and that in first-class style; for 'Bathybius,' coming in with a bunch of papers, coughing, and looking cruel, began with Sandy's name.

Oh! what a moment is that, after a class-examination, when men have been sitting up week after week, with wet towels on their heads,

grinding fact after fact into their skulls from long
slips, from the margins of text-books, from dirty
notes, from the learning of crammers.   What a
moment! The diligent one who wants to write his
weekly letter home, and to say, by the way, as it
were, 'I had a first-class with "Bathybius" last week.
He is a rum old fellow, but much fairer than "Tissue,"
for I worked a vast deal harder for *him* and didn't
even get a fifty per cent.   There's a good deal of
cheating goes on.   I hear that a fellow who got
a hundred per cent., is somehow connected with
an old fellow-student of "Tissue's"—old Spens, the
baronet and occulist—and for that reason he got
a hundred per cent.'—the diligent one does not
like his name to be omitted from the list, and
blames his professor for cheating.

Haco, for a moment, felt that Sandy must be
favoured, when having heard 'Tissue' in the morning, he came up to Nicolson Street to hear 'Bathybius,' in the afternoon, say:

'The papers, on the whole, are very fair—very fair indeed. One student, however, is *facile princeps*—(loud applause)—*facile princeps*. (Sustained applause, going on for two-minutes-and-a-half, during which period 'Bathybius' looks at his watch, the examination papers, and the door.) Now that is about enough. Mr Alexander Baxter has obtained ninety-nine—and—a—half—of—all —the—available—marks. (Uproarious applause, to which there seems to be no end. 'Bathybius' eyeing the 'femur' of a walrus ferociously, as if he would greatly like to seize it and descend among the benches, using it as a lethal weapon.' Ninety-nine—and—a—half—of—all—the—available—marks. I debated somewhat with myself and my assistant upon that half mark. I weighed it; I considered it; I turned it upside down. It all depended upon a colon or semi-colon. Had Mr Baxter written colon, he would have lost the half mark; writing semi-colon, he obtained it. (Huge tramping of feet, kept up till clouds of dust rise from the rear benches of the class-room.) I am familiar with the fact that the ancestral ape is the head of the family tree here. Quite so. Yes. I see him, poor fellow, smirking on your lips, grinning in your faces, grinding in your hoofs. Poor fellow! Yes, you are a disgrace to him. He would not own you. He would, if he were alive, cut you off with a nut—a small hazel nut, nothing larger than that. (Suddenly bundling up all the examination papers, with one brief, decisive glance at the door and two ridges of contempt on the sides of his face; whence instantaneous silence. Papers laid down again and the beginnings of a smile.) After all, gentlemen, perhaps he would have only cut you off with cocoa-nut, which, I may say, is a larger fortune than ever I had when I began the world. (Renewed indication of applause and clouds of dust in the back benches. Bundling of examination papers begun again.) Ninety-nine-

and-a-half per cent., Mr Baxter. Next paper—
seventy-two, Mr Moy. I am disappointed in Mr
Moy. I thought from the indications of attention
given by him that he would have obtained more.
The remaining names are '——And the professor,
rapidly reading through a long list of second-class
names, pushed them aside, and opened fire upon the
animal kingdom which had promoted themselves
from blubber to backbone.

The upshot of it was, however, that Sandy
Baxter had immensely distinguished himself; and
Haco approached him, almost hat in hand, that
afternoon, congratulated him, and asked him if he
would care to come down the Firth with Lady
Mary Hay, some sick children, and himself, at the
end of the week.

Sandy was like Christie—honours made him
modest. The more he had of them, the less he
seemed to care about them; the more careful he
was not to look 'cocky' and conceited. There

may have been a higher kind of cockiness in the quiet assumption that ninety-nine-and-a-half per cent. was his birthright; but if there was, it was not a cockiness which offended any one like loud brag or condescending ways, or the superior appearance of genius cultivated by many persons who get fewer marks than Sandy.

'You certainly are an awful swell, Sandy,' said Haco, humbly, who, though he expected to come into his father's surgical baronetcy, did not feel that the distant prospect of such an honour entitled him to feel himself on a level with the son of his father's grieve.

'I don't know,' said Sandy; 'maybe there are a hundred or two gomerals competing with me;' and he promised he would patronize Haco's yacht, not saying it would be patronage, though Haco felt it would be.

*　　*　　*　　*　　*

Lady Mary's ten children were at the end of Granton Harbour on the morning when the two students were to meet them. It was a magnificent forenoon, with the light of the sun well shaded by clouds which did not promise to blow hard during the day. But the wind which did blow was towards the west instead of towards the east. It blew inside instead of outside the Firth, and Sandy suggested that if they were to sail safely and comfortably, they could do it better up than out of the Firth. The ten children were pale-faced objects; three of them on crutches; three of them with slings, in which their pinched arms reposed; four of them with bands, belts, or bandages arranged round them. They looked from Sandy to Haco with expectant, anxious faces, as they discussed the wind, and, presently, when Lady Mary came down the pier, from a house where she had been making a visit, they rushed at her as if to a mother, gathered round her in a

group, and lugged her towards Sandy and Haco.
They went down a slippery stair to the yacht, and,
as the tide was running up and down with a
treacherous appearance of green suction, which set
the tangles waving, Haco received the children in
his arms as Sandy passed them down. It was
Haco's inestimable privilege, also, to lift Lady
Mary in his arms and to place her on the deck of
his own yacht. She felt as if a hero had just
rescued her from drowning; he, as if the kind
gods had left him nothing better to live for.

They drew out of the harbour very rapidly and
into the Firth.

'It would be pleasanter to go up,' said Haco.

'Up towards Alloa?' said Lady Mary.

'Yes.'

'Strawfield is not at home. Now that I think
of it, we might do worse than take the children
there. We shall get them something nice to eat
and drink.'

'What do you say, mate?' asked Haco, looking from the tiller to the bow.

'Say?'

'Yes.'

'I think we will run up nicely with this wind; and if we're not to hit it off on the Strawfield side, we're sure of a meal on the Binkie side, anyway.'

'Do you mean if the wind is contrary, Mr Baxter?'

'Just so, my lady.'

'Not that we may not be welcome at Straw-field?'

'I didn't think of that.'

'Up the Firth it is,' cried Haco, peremptorily, as he had a right to do, being skipper. 'Up the Firth it is.'

And Sandy being at the ropes, the yacht swung to the wind and made off in the direction pro-posed. The children began clapping their hands, and exchanged opinions in that broken tongue which was, probably, the language of Paradise. The Firth was good to them. It did not tumble them about. It did not sicken them. It did not drench them with spray. The farther they sailed the louder they spoke, and as they came in sight of Strawfield, hours after, Lady Mary, looking at Haco, said,

'You are my brother to-day. You could not have devised anything for me that I could so much have appreciated.'

CHAPTER XI

RECRUITING

THE Spray did her very best after she left Granton Harbour. The breeze was not very strong, but it seemed to have force enough to propel a thousand yachts up the Firth at a great rate. It carried them beyond the Artillery Buoy, Cramond Isle, Queensferry, and distant parts above, till they arrived opposite Lady Mary's brother's place. The children were a little bewildered and shy at first. There was no reason why they should have been so. Each of them had been through Lady Mary's hand in the hospital, and was familiar with her presence in the wards; all of them knew Haco by sight; some of them had seen Sandy. Sandy, however, did not encourage their approaches; he thought they were apt to be a little too familiar; and when a boy near him with a crutch asked what the red buoy was, after they had cleared out of Granton, Sandy did not answer. He looked upon it as an impertinence. He was of opinion that the children ought to whisper. Perhaps he was offended because they opened fire upon him first of all, being of a commoner type than Haco and Lady Mary. Anyhow, he did not like it, and he did not answer the little boy with the crutch, and his silence made the children keep their lips closed all the way up to Cramond. By that time, however, the salt air had got into their blood; the original wickedness which was in them began to assert itself, and they laughed and clapped their hands, and asked questions of each other, Haco, and Lady Mary, without any respect of persons.

Her ladyship was, at first, a little nervous, going up the Firth. She was afraid they might meet her brother's yacht. She concluded, however, that he would not have his yacht there at that time of the year. Indeed, he might be making speeches in the House of Lords. If so, so much the better. Apart from that, she enjoyed the sail very much, and sitting beside Haco in the stern, she smiled and laughed at the little reports of the children's speeches he brought her from time to time. They were all very rosy in the face, when, hours later, the yacht cast anchor opposite her brother's mansion. There was a little difficulty about getting ashore, but Haco said there need be none;  so Lady Mary, clinging to him, with her arms round his neck, allowed him to wade on to a very nice beach, to which all the children were taken, one after another being brought ashore very like

Lady Mary. They ate a great deal of the material set down to them by Sandy and Haco; then they began crawling on all-fours to look for shells; such specimens as they got being presented to Haco, who knew nothing about them, and then to Sandy, who could answer any question about anything, as if he had been the Admirable Bain, successor to Crichton, of the same capacity. By-and-bye, having eaten their luncheon, they showed a desire to disperse in the wood, and Lady Mary was left alone with Haco, Sandy having followed the young ones.

'We shall not have time to sail back. My brother is in London. I shall get a loan of as many conveyances as will carry us all back. You can send a man round for the yacht from Granton afterwards.'

'All right,' said Haco, happy in Lady Mary's presence, and understanding that it was the last time he would see her before she left for Vienna.

' How they scream, to be sure!' said Lady Mary.

' Yes; they are enjoying themselves.'

' I shall be sorry to leave them.'

' Yes, I suppose you will.'

' Poor things, they grow into one's heart!'

' I suppose they do. Look at that little rascal with the crutch belabouring his little cousin with the broken arm—— Ah! good! there's Sandy.'

' A sign of health.'

' A vigorous sign.'

' I go to Vienna this week.'

' I am sorry you are going.'

' Yes; I think you are.'

' Very sorry.'

' Perhaps the only one who really cares.'

' That's impossible.'

' No; not so impossible as you think.'

' You are universally—versally—loved.'

' Liked—not loved. There is a difference. I love to be liked; I do not like to be loved.'

'1 do not understand.'

'No?'

'No.'

'To be liked is to be useful, to be able to do good;
to be loved is to be useless, to be followed about, to
be considered the aim and object—the red artillery
target we have just passed of such as you, Haco.'

'Perhaps.'

'Not perhaps—certainly. I do not care for
love; I appreciate liking.'

'You will be in Vienna for a long time?'

'For years.'

'I shall come to Vienna.'

'To study?'

'To see Lady Mary Hay.'

'Poor Haco? You will learn that I am more
deeply consecrated to my art than you suppose;
that I am invincible; that I cannot be run after
over the face of Europe. Dear Haco, you must

turn in upon your studies, and forget that you
have thought that you have ever cared about me.'

' Forget ? '

' Ah ! the children are joining hands and dancing
under my brother's old trees. See, the master of
ceremonies is Sandy. He knows how to range
them.'

' Sandy knows everything.'

' They trip it very prettily, advancing, retiring,
bowing to each other—ah ! the poor boy with the
crutch !—and Sandy, to judge from the rotundity
of his mouth, whistling a tune to which they go.'

' In three days, then, you go ? '

' In two.'

' To Vienna ? '

' To Vienna.'

' I shall follow.'

' No, Haco, you will not.'

' I shall dream of following.'

' Ah ! '

'Without you, what do you think Edinburgh will be? What do you think the profession will be? Will life be worth living, Mary Hay? It will be too utterly desolate, meaningless and without joy, or anticipation of it. I shall go into mourning as if I were a widower.'

'See, the children are dancing down towards us. Children, you will come with me to the housekeeper's room of Strawfield. She does not expect us, but she is always prepared for emergencies, and this is an emergency she will enjoy. Haco, the sky is getting dark with clouds. The sun has retired from view. The Firth has risen. I was right, I think, in suggesting that we should, all of us, drive back. What do you think, Mr Baxter?'

'I'm ready for any emergency, like the housekeeper.'

'Well, let us all go up together. Haco?'

'Yes.'

'Haco, when I have gone to Vienna, you will work at your profession ?'

'I shall try.'

'You will—— Ah, the housekeeper! My dear Mrs Donaldson, this is rather a visitation.'

'Lady Mary, there is nobody at home. We can take you all in. I hope, dear heart, you are well ?'

'Yes, thanks. Have you carriages to spare ?'

'I think so. We have carts, at any rate, for these.'

'For *these ?*'

'Yes, your ladyship.'

'"Inasmuch as"—— You know the rest.'

'Yes, your ladyship.'

'Very well; find carriages; we do not return by yacht. My brother has not been home lately ?'

'He is going round the world.'

'Globe-trotting ?'

'Yes, your ladyship.'

'I thought he had gone to the House of Lords to air his views—chiefly against us, Mrs Donaldson, for he hates me for throwing over the traditions of the family and becoming a nurse—a nun —a sister—a practitioner. Yes, yes, the little ones only want a little green grass, a few trunks of trees, and a glint of the shine of the sun, to find abundant amusement. Poor little ones! How they laugh! How they crow! How much they find to amuse each other in looking round a moss-covered stem and meeting, eye to eye, and face to face! I cannot look on their enjoyment with dry eyes, now I am leaving them.'

'But, my lady, you will have children of your own.'

'Never, never.'

'Oh, do not speak as if you had taken a vow of celibacy. Never is a long word.'

'Never.'

'My lady, I will call them all in, and the gentlemen, too, and you will have carriages home to Edinburgh, and God bless you!'

'I shall say "Good-bye" to Haco, and stay at home one night before I set out to Vienna. Haco speak to me aside.'

CHAPTER XII

THE SPENS SPLINT

FEW things are more difficult in life than getting into a passion with propriety. Propriety presupposes a certain amount of reflection in the person who affects it, and the essence of passion is explosion. Sir Thomas Spens, when crossed, irritated, and roused, was nothing if not an explosive force. It was not good for anybody to be near him when he was thus affected, and Haco felt that one day, after the summer session came to an end and he had returned to Binkie.

The end of the Session brought nothing new to
Haco. He had stood fairly well in his classes—
that is, he was on the lists, though low down, while
Sandy got both the medals. But he was otherwise
provoking to his father, for it had been coming out
week after week, that he had contracted large
debts.

At first Sir Thomas said nothing about them.
When a tailor sent in a large bill, he paid it without comment; Haco, at the time, being at Christie's
in Forfarshire. Then a manufacturer of philosophical instruments sent in a bill for a microscope
and endless specimens, and for other articles in
steel and brass remotely connected with the summer
studies.

To these he said 'Pshaw!' as he paid them.

Presently in came a collection of bills from book-
sellers; five of them, one after another, each bigger
than its neighbour.

'Pshaw! pshaw!' said Sir Thomas on that occasion.

Accounts came in from a furnishing decorator, and a dealer in articles of vertu, from a dealer in marine stores, and a manufacturer of compasses, from a hatter, and a fruiterer, a jeweller, and a stationer.

'Pshaw! pshaw! pshaw! This is too much of a good thing!' said the baronet, rising from the perusal of the bills, and witnessing the shedding of cheques like leaves in Vallombrosa. 'Too much of a good thing! Why, the lad has been living at the rate of six hundred pounds a-year! — six positive, individual hundred pounds a-year! He seems to have been buying everything that his eye saw. Haco! Haco!'

At the time, Haco was in the garden. He was finding it rather lonely. Sandy had not come over for holidays; he was taking his holidays with a pupil who was travelling in the Highlands, and who kept up some of his summer studies.

'Isaac! Isaac!' shouted the baronet, when his son did not respond to his summons.

Isaac put in an alarmed head. He knew that Sir Thomas had some preparations of the tail ends of the nerve at the back of the eyeball of a mole, on glass slides, about which he was acutely anxious. He hoped nothing had occurred to them like the tumbling of the bottle of nitric acid one day over the same nerves in the back of the eyeball of a bat, which Sir Thomas declared had cost him the labour of years.

'The labour of years, you reckless, heedless, misguided fool of sixty!' cried the baronet, looking at the ruined filaments on the slides and at the open mouth of his henchman.

'It was an accident, Sir Thomas,' said Isaac. 'I didn't observe there was a stopper in the bottle, and that it contained nitric acid. Now, the con-

tents of any other bottle would have passed over
the surface of the slide harmless. I'm regretful
that our experiment should have come to such
an untimely conclusion.   But there are plenty
more bats hanging by their feet under the branches
o' the trees. I can get ye a dizzen any nicht.
An' I do not like to be reminded o' my years in
that passionate manner, Sir Thomas Spens.'

Grief closed the baronet's mouth on that occasion,
and he waved his servant from the room.   On the
present occasion, however, he kept on,

'Isaac! Isaac! bring my son here, will you?'

And Isaac, hastening into the garden, searched
for Haco, and warned him that he was afraid his
father had something disagreeable to say to him.

'Disagreeable!' said Haco, abandoning a book
and rising from a sheltered arbour. 'What is that
for, Isaac?   What have I been doing?'

'I couldn't really say, sir; but there are letters
on the table, and the cheque-book's out.   He's been

tearin' away at them all mornin', Mr Haco, and I think—yes, I think he's a little tired of it. But you'll see for yourself, sir.'

Haco went into the study, and saw his father on his hearthrug. His cheque-book was in his hand, or, rather, the boards of the book, for the cheques were all torn out of it. Sir Thomas grasped the empty volume with every symptom of aggravated disdain.

' Oh, you are there—eh ? eh ? '

' Yes, father. What is it ? '

' What is it, sir ? '

' Yes, father.'

' It's that ! ' said Sir Thomas, holding out the exhausted cheque-book. ' Do I own a sugar mill, sir ? Am I a brewery ? Am I a pilfering but opulent retail trader ? '

' How do you mean, father ? '

' Eh ? eh ? What do you think I am ? I'm not Croesus, hang you ! Eh ? eh ? '

And, for sheer lack of language, Sir Thomas'
cheeks swelled, and the veins in his brow grew
large, and his eyes gathered an expression of fiery
vehemence in them which Haco had not seen there
before.

'You're very well off, aren't you, father? I
always thought you were. You never said you
weren't.'

'Very well off, sir! Do you suppose a practising
surgeon can retire with a limitless fortune? Do
you think that the profession you have adopted
is a paying profession—that it is anything else
than the hardest worked and the most badly-remunerated profession in the world?'

'What did you send me into it for, then?'

'The most badly-remunerated profession in the
world, in which there is no honour to be got, as at
the Church or the Bar, and on which there are cast
innumerable gibes and insults from a world of idiots
—idiots who despise the doctor till they want him,

then run for him, and malign him when they
recover. Why, you young fool, I am a poor man,
and you are drawing on me to the extent of six
hundred pounds a-year! It's '—— so and so, and
so and so, and so and so. For Sir Thomas burst
into stronger language, and sustained it for some
time, than was for the good of young folk to
hear.

Haco was terribly disturbed. He did not know
how to feel, how to look, how to answer his father.
He stood twisting his fingers, and thinking what
a want of personal taste there was in this
demonstration of rough anger.

'Why, father,' he answered, when Sir Thomas
gasped to find his breath, 'you don't know all my
responsibilities, the sort of things I needed to buy,
and all that.'

Sir Thomas went on gasping, and thumped the
dull boards of the cheque-book together.

'I am robbed, sir—literally and positively robbed

of three hundred pounds! You shall have fifty
pounds to get along on next session, and see how
you like it! Fifty pounds, sir, to teach you
economy—to show you how many a poor fellow
has the battle of life to fight; fifty pounds to
educate you!'

'I can't positively do it on that,' said Haco,
thinking of Roger and the weekly bill of
mortality.

'I did it on less, sir; I did it on less. Eh? eh?
You can't, positively? Hang it, you are a born
fool! Look at that!' And again the boards of
the exhausted cheque-book drearily flapped against
each other. 'You will oblige me by sitting down
and giving me a succint account of the year—of
the entire year, from October to August—with
every item of expenditure which has brought
robbery upon me.'

'My dear father, I couldn't do that to save my

life. I positively thought you said to me that it
didn't matter—that I might order what I required.'

'No doubt. On three hundred a-year you might
order anything— anything that you required —
anything that an undergraduate had the least
necessity to buy. Now, I insist upon it—a full
account of the year, from October to August.'

Sir Thomas tossed his cheque-book afar off. It
fell with a dull thud at the skeleton feet of a
skunk, shook the skunk's fore-paws, and flapped
wide open.

'A whole year!' said Haco, turning his eyes up
to the roof. 'Well, father, not much has happened
in it. I hope I can tell you it all. I don't know
whether you will think I ought to be excused on
the back of it; but, if you will listen attentively,
there's no reason why I should not say what I
have experienced. I have sung songs about it.
Some of it has been intense—utter—consummate.
I have been reading dear Mr Ruskin, and I must

use the phrases which belong to my knowledge.
From October —— Yes. Well, October was a
wretched month. I just passed my preliminary.
I knew nobody. I had not matriculated. I had
not met Lady Mary Hay. I had not been introduced to Dr Crum. I had not seen Professor
Stewart. I had not bought a book. I had not
bought an instrument. I had not been in the
college library. I had not seen an old school-
fellow. I had not '——

'For Heaven's sake, Haco, do not be so prosy
and literary. Do not be literary. Be scientific.
Be accurate, precise, downright. But do not spin
it out so long.'

'Father, you are unreasonable.'

Sir Thomas sat down and folded his hands, and
seemed inclined to close his eyes. It was a hopeful
symptom. Haco saw that his wrath was exhausted.

'My education,' said Haco, 'has been wholly

scientific, though my tastes are, probably, artistic. Tree—oh, Tree says they are altogether artistic.'

'Tree has been your ruin,' said Sir Thomas.

'No, father, Tree is the best of men. He is like Dr Dale and Dr Crum—much misunderstood. If the Royal Academicians would just agree to consider that Tree's nerves are different from theirs, and that the "To Pan" pulls them to different issues, I can assure you, father, they would soon learn that Tree should be received among them, as one of themselves, without surprise. I regard Tree as a brother.'

'I asked you to give me an account of your year. I want to know who the ruffians are who have been plucking the pigeon—the poor, self-satisfied pigeon, who thinks he knows everything. Answer me!'

'I am answering you. But I must submit my opinions as I go along. Tree deserves to have an

LL.D. given him. He has more artistic culture than any of the professors.'

'Hang it!' shouted Sir Thomas, getting off his chair, rising and walking to the skunk for his cheque-book, 'I have asked you for the details of your expensive year at college, and you offer me elaborate opinions about who deserve degrees —honorary, honourable degrees. Who is Tree? We might as well give these letters to a war correspondent, with the indefinite prospect of obtaining from him the best military history in Europe. Why, sir, he would forthwith sit down upon his degree and think he had written it.'

Haco thought his father was cooling, and proceeded:

'Well, father, I will try not to be literary, but to be scientific, and to let you know exactly how it has been spent. I have had a very good landlady, who has not overcharged me. You could not grumble at her accounts, on the whole. They

have been very reasonable—very much so, indeed.
She is a little superstitious, but not a cheat. Many
of my fellow-students have been cheated, but not
I. No. Even Sandy Baxter's landlady '——

'Who is Sandy Baxter?'

'Sandy Baxter?'

'Yes.'

'Do you not know about him?'

'Would I ask you if I did?'

'Why, your grieve's son—the ablest man at the
University of Edinburgh.'

'The—the—tawny boy with the inquiring eyes?
Eh? eh?'

'Yes, father.'

'At the University?'

'Yes.'

'Studying medicine?'

'Yes.'

'In the same classes with you?'

'Yes.'

' My grieve's son ? '

' Yes.'

In—the—same—— Isaac! Isaac!'

' Yes, Sir Thomas.'

' Throw out these mutilated nerves.'

' Yes, Sir Thomas.'

' I have not heard of this before.'

' I didn't think of telling you.'

' Does this young man understand—my—splint ? '

' Which one ? '

' Ah! which one, to be sure! that is a sign of intelligence on your part, poor pigeon! The Spens splint. Does he understand the Spens splint ? The splint you placed upon the foreleg of the pony when it was fractured by the hind leg of my mare ? '

' How do you mean, father ? '

' Is it possible that you did not apply that splint ? '

' What splint ?

'The splint upon the pony's leg. Isaac! Isaac!'

'Yes, Sir Thomas.'

'Send for Baxter at once, and bring him here.'

'What do you want him for?'

'I want him to see what I have got for a son—yes, for a surgical son and successor. Haco, I will make a physician of you. You are not fit for anything else. Only as a physician will you be able to hold up your head with the world. You are your mother's son, alas! I thought you had inherited the taste. But no! I see it all now. The grieve's son applied the splint. He is the surgeon; you are the fool. You shall be a physician.'

CHAPTER XIII

UNEXHAUSTED ANGER

Having finished his interview with his son, Sir Thomas Spens rose and walked out of the Manor into the fields. He was in a violent rage, and, at his time of life, that is an expensive luxury. He was much too good a pathologist not to know that it would not do for his ancient heart to exaggerate its beating beyond a certain point; that in the case of its jumping too violently inside him he might tumble, and the heart might not take up its duties again. He was too much used to death to fear it much; still, he did not wish to die, so he judiciously expended all his emotion upon the tops of thistles; and, as he walked, his stick whirled to right and left, and little clouds of down floated in the air.

The truth was, he was as angry with himself as with his son. He began to think that, between his bats, his moles, his owls, and his prolonged experiments upon their eyesight, he might have neglected this son of his. Perhaps he had not put himself to the trouble of finding out what his nature really was, and whether he was fitted for this surgical work for which he had cut him out. That might be, and if it were so, it was none the less provoking to him.

His stick whistled to right and left, the thistle heads fell, the down flew about, and it was only at the proper moment that Mr Baxter's head showed itself at the other side of a wall.

What Sir Thomas wanted and required was a

victim, and here was his grieve, apparently doing nothing in particular—the grieve, who had a son who was on the fair way to become a brilliant surgeon, whereas Haco Spens, on his own showing, was an ass.

'Ah, Baxter,' said the baronet, with so much suppressed anger that his grieve mistook his tone for one of mild cordiality,

'Fine weather for leading and driving, sir,' said the grieve, resting his arms upon a stile and looking over the baronet's head to a field of yellow grain, where a man was sharpening a scythe upon a stone, and a little crowd of women were gathering the cut grain, binding it, and building the sheaves into 'stooks.'

'I daresay. Very fine ; very fine, indeed.'

'There'll be no cause for complaint this year, sir, of percentage of bushels to the acre. None.'

'No cause of complaint! No, no. Will you be good enough to tell me, Baxter, who placed that

splint upon the fore leg of that pony in the spring
of the year? Eh? eh?'

The grieve removed his cap and scratched his
head, and, looking into Sir Thomas' face, saw that
he was in a rage—that the cause of the rage was
the discovery that Alexander Baxter's son had
more brains than his own.

'Eh? eh?'

'There's no cause for anger, sir.'

'No?'

'No, sir.'

'But what if I say there is cause for anger—
deep and vital cause for it? What if I say that
I have never in my life had greater reason to
rise up in my wrath and crush a few people?'

And Sir Thomas, forgetting for a little the
pathology of his heart, allowed his face to become
suffused with the pulses of anger before he turned
savagely upon the thistles and smote them, hip and
thigh. The grieve adjusted his cap and walked off'

with a tremendous width of stride. When Sir Thomas turned, he saw him thirty yards away, and though he shouted 'Baxter! Baxter!' after him, he would not resume his conversation. He seemed preternaturally busy about something far in advance of him.

The baronet was out of breath now. He stopped whipping the thistles. He looked down into the field of yellow grain, where the man with the scythe was mowing, and the reapers were following his footsteps and picking up the ears. It was a pretty pastoral sight, but it did not soothe him. He walked straight on to the Mains, and was presently standing in the doorway, while Mrs Baxter, with a large linen apron on, stood ladling jam into pots. A young lady was sitting at the end of the table addressing the skins which covered the pots. It was all black currant jam, and she was writing that down. Sir Thomas seemed to have seen the girl before, but he was not sure. He half-inclined his head to her, however, as he roughly asked Mrs Baxter,

'Well, ma'am, well, where's that paragon of yours? Will you tell me that?'

His rage had not subsided. Mrs Baxter, startled, dropped her ladle into the jam, and wiped her mouth, after which she made a rather awkward 'cheese' to him.

'Where is he, ma'am?'

'Is it Alexander, Sir Thomas?'

'Is that his name?'

'Is it my husband you would see?'

'No, not particularly; no, at this moment it's your paragon—your surgical genius—the fellow who put up the splint—your son, ma'am.'

'Oh, Sandy, poor fellow! He's away in the Hielands, travelling with a pupil. He'll not be back for some weeks, I believe.'

'He's travelling in the Highlands, is he? You've sent him to the University, ma'am.'

'No, Sir Thomas.'

'I tell you, you have. No equivocation to me. You've given him a college education. You're giving it him now. Don't deny it. He's distinguishing himself, ma'am. He's taking medals. He understands my splint. He set it up in the spring of the year. D—— me, ma'am, don't deny it; but I've been fooled all this time. I thought it was my son's handiwork. I find now it was yours. That's a pretty state of matters, isn't it? I believe I gave it as my opinion that your son would be leading a useful and healthy life if he took up the plough as a profession. Do you understand me, ma'am—the plough?'

Mrs Baxter pursed her lips, took up a pot, and began ladling the jam, as if there were no Sir Thomas there at all.

'I believe, ma'am, I see medals on your mantelpiece. I do see medals—one—two—three—four—five of them in a row.'

He spoke as if he saw five unpopular insects crawling upon her gown.

'I believe you do, sir,' said Mrs Baxter, pride mantling in her eye as she raised her ladle aloft. 'These are what my son Sandy has taken within the year—five medals, Sir Thomas.'

'And you think it's all right, I suppose?'

'I do, sir.'

'But I tell you it's all wrong.'

'I don't see it, Sir Thomas.'

'No; and I'll be bound to say my grieve don't see it, either.'

'He was scared enough at first about it; but Sandy has taught him, Sir Thomas, to look after his own business, and Sandy will look after his.'

'Oh, indeed! And who is this young lady labelling the jam?'

'Surely, Sir Thomas, this is Tibbie Baxter.'

'What! your daughter?'

'My daughter, sir—a grown girl now.'

'I presume she has just returned from an expensive boarding-school, ma'am. Piano—French—use of the globes—accomplishments—eh? eh?'

Tibbie's face warmed into crimson, and she murmured something which the baronet did not hear.

'I may tell you, Mrs Baxter, that I'm not over-satisfied.'

'Don't you be too hard on him, Sir Thomas.'

'I can't pretend to regulate my temper in the face of provocation like this.'

'But think, sir, of the long time he has been without a mother's care and attention, and love and affection.'

'Well, I suppose that's your fault, not mine.'

'I don't understand you, sir.'

'Then you're a mighty simpleton for your pains. I suppose it depended upon you whether he was to have affection.'

'Poor young fellow, he's always had my esteem

and regard. But since his mother died he has been thrown a great deal upon himself.'

'Who are you talking about?'

'Mr Haco.'

'Then, ma'am, I'm talking about your son, and we are at cross-purposes. You will, perhaps, oblige me by taking possession of the Manor, in the next place—carting your furniture over to it and taking possession. Five medals! And my son a fool!'

Sir Thomas went out into the farmyard, where a bantam crowed in his face, though he shook his stick at it, and wandered away to a gate where he searched the horizon for the grieve. But the grieve kept out of his road, and there was nothing for it but wandering back again to his house. He had exhausted himself in his anger. He shut himself into his study, and refused to dine with his son. He would not speak to him, at least, for that day. It might do him a little good to be left alone with his reflections. A few bitter hours could do him no harm.

'Isaac, where is he?' he asked, later on in the evening, while the shadows were falling and the sun was going down.

'He's very much overcome, Sir Thomas. I fear he has gone away by himself to grieve among the trees, with a book in his hand.'

'Very good.'

In the twilight, however, Sir Thomas let himself out of the side of his garden and sauntered among the trees behind the bay where Haco's yacht was. He had not gone far before he heard suppressed girlish laughter, and Haco's unrestrained voice cheerfully exclaiming,

'There, Tibbie, now! that was pretty good, wasn't it? I cut down a whole bushel with that sweep of the scythe.'

Sir Thomas looked from behind an elm, and saw his son manipulating a weighty scythe among a

field of wheat, and close behind him, out of range
of the sweep of the instrument, stooped the young
lady he had seen labelling the jam in the afternoon.
It was disappointing to him. He had hoped his
son was sorry. He had expected him to be wandering up and down, absorbed, with a dismal
foreboding of evil in his mind, and resolutions
formed for economy and hard work against a
coming session. But no! In the sound of his
voice there was nothing but gay cheerfulness as he
went on conversing with the girl at his feet.

'Now I've cut enough, Tibbie. You show me
how to bind it up, will you ?'

'Oh, it's quite easy,' said the young lady. 'You
just take a handful of wheat this way—look. Now
you twist this way till it holds like a rope, and
now you lay it on the ground and lift the wheat
on it, this way ; then you gather the ends together.
Oh, my ! there was a nettle stung me just now.
You gather the ends together, and twist, and twist,

and twist, and shove the tail of it under—and there's a sheaf.'

'How pastoral! how innocent!' murmured Sir Thomas. 'It would make everything complete if it were to turn out that that girl was making eyes at my son and meant to marry him—the fool!'

Haco stooped, and, from his point of view at the elm, the baronet saw nothing more. He was sure, however, that there was something worth seeing; so he ascended the bank at the stile, and from a high vantage-ground looked down upon his son's doings. They were not very serious; he was only helping Tibbie to tie up another sheaf, but their heads were very close.

'So!' said Sir Thomas, sarcastically; and the heads went apart, and the sheaf fell to pieces, and Haco stood up confronting his father.

'And this is the young lady who was engaged upon the jam. Have you been long my son's instructor in the agricultural arts?'

'Oh, father! this is only Tibbie—Tibbie Baxter, Sandy's sister. Come and let me introduce you to father, Tibbie.'

Sir Thomas bowed elaborately; Tibbie curtseyed, and seemed inclined to walk off. She did not, however, till the baronet remarked that he would like to speak with his son again. She then picked up the scythe and departed, and Haco lounged to the stile.

'It is my profound conviction,' said the father, 'that you have been born without a cerebrum, Haco—that you are an irresponsible creature— that you will shortly die of idiocy and inanition.'

CHAPTER XIV

PROPOSAL OF MARRIAGE

THE autumn holidays unwound themselves slowly at Binkie, and Haco did not enjoy them in the least. Sandy was away all the time. Tibbie mysteriously disappeared; and it was only after indefinite trouble that Haco found out from the housekeeper that she had been sent to Edinburgh to learn dressmaking.

'She is a giddy girl,' said the housekeeper, confidentially, 'who has suddenly turned out quite good-looking on her mother's hands, and who gives herself airs accordingly. It's a sad misfortune for a plain girl to become attractive all of a sudden. It turns their heads, and they think themselves ever so much more valuable than they are. Now, for my part, I wouldn't give a plain girl for a pretty girl, Mr Haco.'

' How's that ? '

' Because they are worth so much more. They can do so many things that the pretty ones can't.'

' Well, I suppose they must. We don't ask the pretty ones to do a great deal. We only want them to send on second, third, fourth, and fifth editions of themselves to posterity, to keep the world smiling.'

' Ah, sir, you don't know what you are talking about. It's them that gives all the trouble—that makes all the mischief. If we had one or two generations of quite ugly women, Mr Haco, the world would be perfect.'

' You think ugliness is morality ? '

' Well, I think it's the angel with the flaming sword which watches over the Seventh Command-ment.'

' You do ? '

' Yes.'

' Then you take a meaner view of the world than I do. Tell Isaac to tell little Waters to put a dish of peaches in the arbour near the west parapet. I'm going to read there.'

Haco meditated much upon the sending away of Tibbie Baxter to Edinburgh. He agreed with the housekeeper that she had quite suddenly turned out to be pretty, and he had come to that time of life when he thought not to be in love was high treason to his nature. He lay in his arbour with his dish of peaches and his book, and looked upon the palpitating Firth and its driving sea-birds, and heard its low monotone of breaking waves, and assured himself, that, certainly, he had a right to be in love. With whom ? With Lady Mary or

Tibbie ? He knew he was in love, but he could
not definitely say with which. Perhaps he would
have been right if he had said with both; but then
that would have been too much of a good thing.
He looked out on the Firth, and told himself that
he had a grand passion for Lady Mary, and a
simple, unaffected love for Tibbie. He loved
Tibbie as he might a pony, or a doe, or a caged
canary ; Lady Mary as a benign goddess who con-
descended to be friendly with him, to interest
herself in his behalf, and to warn him of his
faults. Yet at that point he felt there
was a difference—that his love in the one case
lapsed into veneration, while in the other it
glowed into a familiar fire; where he could lift
Lady Mary's fingers to his lips he could take
Tibbie to his heart. There was a difference. He
did not know what to make of it ; but from starting with the presumption that he had a grand
passion for Lady Mary, he came to the conclusion

that he had a deep respect for her and the deeper
emotion for Tibbie.   After all, was there not something more profoundly romantic in loving a pretty
peasant girl than in giving one's heart to the sister
of an earl ?   There was no self-seeking, no alloy of
selfishness, no pride of the world, in loving Tibbie.
It was emotion pure and simple—the clear well-
spring of affection. Besides, Tibbie never re-
proached him ; she never pointed out the way in
which he ought to go. She never said what he
must do to reach perfection. She was content to
take him as he was—a dreaming student, without
aim and object. On the whole, looking at the
matter from the point of view of his arbour, and
the moaning sea and the spectacle of the city
beyond, he concluded that it was Tibbie who had
his heart, and Lady Mary who had his understanding. He felt sure it was, for he missed the girl as he
went out among the trees and looked up and down
the fields, and heard nothing but the rattle of a stone

upon a scythe and the grieve reprimanding the reapers. Nor did his father's attitude to him decrease his sentiment to her. His father leaped to the conclusion that he was a fool, and went on treating him as such. It was 'Eh? eh?' for ever and a day; not a word of affection, not a syllable of sympathy. Sir Thomas turned his back on him when he spoke; never asked him to witness the progress of his investigations into the eye; never treated him as if he were a student of the sciences at all. He could not recover the episode of the splint, and his irritation at the applause he had falsely bestowed upon Haco. He had no mind to forgive the ridiculous extravagance of his year at college, so he punished him by ignoring him and being rude to him, and letting him know as often as he met him, in house, field, or garden, that he was only worthy of notice to be sneezed at or pooh-poohed.

Haco may have deserved that treatment, but

it sent him across the Firth a week or two before
the beginning of a new session, with some bitterness in his disposition towards the author of his
being, and with a quiet craving for sympathy. That
was not lessened by the difficulties which again
met him at Queen Street. Mrs Ramsay was
surprised to hear him say that he had not liked
her forwarding bills of arrears to Sir Thomas.

'Deary me, Mr Spens, sir, what is it to the like
of your father, the matter of a few pounds, when
my husband, the bank messenger, has never been
able to get employment again?'

'I don't believe you have a husband, Mrs
Ramsay,' said Haco, who had never seen or heard
him speak, though he was a subject of incessant
allusion to Mrs Ramsay. It was not convenient
for her to discuss the subject any longer, so she
left him to pursue an accumulation of letters,
among them a little heap of Roger's demands for
arrears which had crept up in the interval. Haco

had been so impressed with his father's coolness,
that though he had been sent back to college with
an undiminished allowance, he determined to make
heroic efforts to retrench. He had a great mind,
at the outset of the session, to put the whole case
in a lawyer's hand, as Sandy had long before
advised him. Then he shrank from it under
the old feeling of cowardice at being confronted
in public with the man's death, and at a certain
softness at his heart, which told him that in
feeding the dead man's orphans he was engaged
in a good thing. Still, the sight of the letters
vexed him terribly, and he felt the weight of a
literal millstone round his neck as he read them.

The first night of his return, he strolled up to the
Mound to see Tree. He found Tree in his studio,
with Professor Stewart, a couple of editors, and one
or two aged nondescripts, with spectacles on their
noses. Tree had not much time to give to him.
He was diligently attempting to sell one or two of

his pictures, and he was giving a private view of another, and entertaining Professor Stewart at large.

The professor had only returned from the Highlands, and was the hue of bronze, and tossed his plaid about him with the strength of a Shetland pony throwing his superfluous mane off his eyes. He recognised Haco at once, and, neglecting the purchasers, he came round to him among the easels, shouting'

'Spens, Spens! Back to college! Understand me, now—my house is open to you. Let me see, you are a member of the " Hellenic ?"'

'No, Professor Stewart; I am sorry to say I am only a member of the Blue Pill Society, which reads a paper once a-week during the winter session.'

'Blue Pill Society! Now, that's a mistake. A man like you, with golden hair a maid of eighteen might be proud of, should take his recreation in some other way. You can't read Greek ?'

' Not very well.'

' Well, come and sit and look like a Greek There are a few of us snuffy old codgers who wil be very glad to see you; and if you can't make much of a cobbled chorus, never mind; you can give us " Sir Patrick " afterwards in your best style. The Blue Pill Society! It's enough to make any boy aged before he's born. I don't approve of these institutions at all. The Man in the Iron Mask is all very well for an argument or whether Wallace would have achieved the independence of Scotland single-handed, if Warren hadn't given him up; or whether it is better in church to have music produced through the nose or assisted by an organ;—all these questions are very well—very well, Spens. But Blue Pills!'

' I don't like them.'

' Quite right. Neither stomachically nor by way of argument ought you to like them.'

' It's cruel, besides, I think.'

' Cruel to the man who swallows them ? '

' Or to the beasts.'

' Beasts ? How d'ye mean ? '

' As far as I know, they are only given to beasts. Why, Professor Stewart, it would make your heart bleed to see Kendrick's back-yard. I should say Kendrick was a little mercenary, and rather soft-hearted, but by no means cruel. Well, his back-yard is full of street-dogs. One dog hasn't got a tail; Kendrick has whipped it off with a knife. Another dog hasn't got a left eye ; Kendrick has seared it out with a hot iron. A third hasn't got a left fore-paw; Kendrick has amputated it. A fourth hasn't got an entire skull ; Kendrick has chipped it like an egg, and removed a bit of brain, to see the brute dance a physiological waltz. A fifth has a tube right through the side into his liver. A sixth wears his heart on his sleeve. It is sickening, Professor Stewart.

I hate it—I loathe it. I do not believe they dis-
cover anything.'

'Poor Spens! you are very much in earnest.
Look in at the "Hellenic." We can do better for
you than that. Now, Tree, Tree, my dear fellow,
you are selling that picture dirt cheap. I know
your friend with the spectacles. It's William
Idson, a man with a dirty chimney, and more
guineas than he can count. Idson, don't you pretend that Tree's view from your front door is
only worth four hundred pounds; it's worth four
times four hundred, and it's all very easy for you
to heap up money at the back of your counter.
Any man with a blunt conscience and a trade can
do it; but he can't paint Tree's pictures. Tree
don't give it him under eight hundred.'

They were bargaining when Haco went out.

Sandy was to be at his rooms that night. He
would go up and see him. So to Buccleuch Place
he set off. He had no great anxiety about seeing

Sandy; but he thought he might hear about Tibbie—how she came to be in Edinburgh; where she was working: how she liked it.

It was greatly to his delight when he knocked at the door to have it opened by Tibbie, who was dressed in a tight-fitting carmine-coloured gown, and who looked ten times more good-looking than ever he had seen her.

She showed him into Sandy's room, her eyes sparkling, and as she closed the door she said,

'Sandy's landlady has a sister sick in the Potter's Row, and she thought it would save a doctor's fee if he would look at her. They have just gone off together. I am keeping house for them.'

'Well, Tibbie, I am mighty glad to see you.'

'You couldn't be more pleased than I am, Mr Haco.'

'Tibbie, drop the "mister." It is really time you called me Haco, as Sandy does. I am delighted to

meet you again. You are looking ever so much
better than the last time.'

'I think I like living in town.'

'I hope you haven't to work hard, Tibbie?'

'Not very, and it's nice work. I made all Lady
Mary Hay's bodices, and packed them for her to
Vienna.'

'I say!'

'Yes, indeed I did. She has a waist like '——

'Not like yours, Tibbie.'

'Please not to put your arm round me.'

'Why not?'

'Because they might come in, and I would look
confused; and Sandy wouldn't like it.'

'Oh, bother Sandy!'

'He wouldn't, I assure you.'

'Well, I don't care a snap of my thumb about
Sandy. Do you know, Tibbie, I have made up my
mind to a great resolve.'

'Have you, Haco?'

'Yes.   Can you guess what it is?'

'No, Haco.'

'Tibbie, you can.'

'I cannot, indeed, unless it is that you are to unwind your arms and let me sit free at the table, where I have so much work to do.'

'Tibbie, you are a hypocrite; you know perfectly.   You know that I have missed you dreadfully at Binkie, and that I am greatly in need of some one to look after my purse and to keep house for me.   This is my second year now, and I get into such a lot of trouble, Tibbie—everybody robbing me, and nobody pitying me, and father calling me all the fools; and I want you to be my little wife.'

The colour died away from Tibbie's face; she looked ghastly pale, and leaned heavily on Haco.

'Haco,' she said, 'your father would never forgive you.'

'He doesn't need to know'

' And my father ? '

' Doesn't need to know.'

' And Sandy ? '

' Bother Sandy.'

' And my mother ? '

' She would be quite pleased, I'm sure. I'm a tremendous favourite of hers. She would like having me for a son-in-law. And I know this, Tibbie, that if I had you for a wife, sitting opposite me in the evenings when I came home from college, I should work a great deal better. It would be the making of me. Tibbie, say you will be my wife.'

' Haco, you are not serious.'

' I am.'

' No, you are not. You are trying to make a fool of me '—tears.

' Tibbie, I have been thinking all autumn that I should greatly like to have you for my wife— that it would make all the difference in the world

to me. We can do it in this way; I can take you
to a Sheriff's and sign something in his office, and
it is all right, we are man and wife. Why, Tibbie,
I have three hundred a-year. I am sure many a
man marries on less.'

Tibbie sobbed outright and clutched his arm, and
said,

'Oh, Haco! Your father—your father! What
would he say?'

'It isn't what he would say, Tibbie; it's what
you would say. I consider that he has forfeited
all title to dictate to me what I should do. He
has been so cold, and rude, and rough, that I must
go my way without thinking about him. He
can't possibly—his human nature couldn't let him
—be one bit rougher if he knew I were married.
You see I have experienced the worst.'

'And Lady Mary, Haco?'

'I shall always esteem her, and admire and
reverence her, at a distance—a great far-off

distance, seeing her as a good angel, a kind of lady abbess of a free order of nuns. She will never marry—at any rate, she will never marry me. Tibbie, believe me, I am bitterly, passionately in earnest. You will come with me to the Sheriff to-morrow or the next day, and no one need know till we choose to tell them.'

' Ah!'

' When we are married I will tell you the history of a great mystery, and perhaps you will help to take me out of it; how, one day, I was the means of depriving a man of his life '——

' Haco!'

' Yes, of his life; and how another man levied two pounds a-week on me on the spot, and keeps it up now, week after week, till I have quarrelled with my father and found life not worth living for vexation.'

' Dear Haco!'

'Dear Tibbie! And you will marry me to-morrow ?'

' Yes.'

'Then am I a saved man, and all will be well.'

CHAPTER XV

AN INCIDENT

A FORTNIGHT passed, and Tibbie went back to her work at the dressmaker's in George Street, and Haco joined his classes. Haco thought over his suggestion about marriage, and came to the conclusion that he had done a wise thing in proposing to Tibbie. He did not look into the future and ask himself what would come of it. He only felt that he greatly wanted affectionate companionship in his studies, and that, under the circumstances,

he had better marry Tibbie. He consulted Mrs
Ramsay about it.

'Mrs Ramsay,' he said, 'I will have to give up
my rooms and go.'

'What ?'

'Yes; I am very sorry; but I am incurring new
responsibilities, and, really, your terms are very
high.'

'Two pounds a-week, Mr Spens. That is really
very little for the rooms you have, and the view.
You can see your dear father's manor in the distance, with a telescope.'

'I would rather not.'

'Well, I can give you a room looking into the
back-yard, with nothing but cats at night and cocks
in the morning. You can have that, Mr Spens, for
sixpence a-week off the rent.'

'Sixpence, Mrs Ramsay! What can I do on the
saving of a sixpence? Can I keep a wife on a sixpence saved ?'

' No, you cannot, Mr Spens.'

' That's just the question, however.'

' Bless the boy, a wife!'

' Yes, a wife—Mrs Haco Spens.'

' I never!'

' On the prospect of marriage, Mrs Ramsay, I begin to be an economist, and I must have something off them, or I will go.'

' Very well, Mr Haco; but I shall feel it my duty to write to Sir Thomas Spens and say to him that you have made a clandestine match. Yes; it's my plain duty to do so.'

' That would be rather shabby.'

' But it would be my duty.'

' It would be awfully shabby, none the less.'

' I have no other option before me, if you insist upon going.'

' Then suppose I stay?'

' Suppose!'

'Yes—that I keep my rooms and go on paying my two pounds, and bring my wife.'

'What is she like? Is she young, or middle-aged, or old?'

'Young.'

'Is she really young, or does she say she is?'

'Both.'

'She is, and says she is?'

'No, she doesn't need to say it. She is really young—younger than I am.'

Oh, poor thing!'

'You don't need to pity her.'

'No, no, I don't. Youth has its compensations, Mr Haco. But I'm sorry for you in anticipation of what may come.'

'And what do you anticipate?'

'It's not for me to say. But I'd be quite pleased that you should have my rooms at the old price; and if your wife is young I'll not be afraid of her,

and we needn't quarrel. Is she—is she—a lady,
Mr Haco ? '

' Of course.'

' I'm glad of that.'

' Very well, then, I'll bring my wife home one of
these days, and no questions will be asked by Mrs
Ramsay ? '

' None.'

Haco met Tibbie on the North Bridge one day.
She was carrying a dress home to somebody, and
being clad in a cloak of homespun, she looked
plainer than usual. But he did not think so.

' Ah, Tibbie ! ' said Haco.

' Yes,' she said, nervously, half-inclined to hurry
on to the end of her journey without further
speech.

' Where are you going ? '

' With a bodice to Moray Place '

' Who to ? '

' A Miss Watson.'

'Give me it.'

She gave it him, and, walking on a few paces, he took out a shilling and presented it to a boy, who promised to convey it to its destination.

'Now, Tibbie, you have plenty of time to come and get married.'

'Haco!'

'Yes, I know all about it. I have been to the Sheriff's, and know how it is done. We only go into a room and sign some papers, and he will ask us one or two questions—then it is all right. I am your husband after that for better or for worse.'

'Haco!'

It took them exactly as long to get married as it would have taken Tibbie to return from Moray Place to her mistress. But they were irrevocably united, none the less.

'You must come to Queen Street, now.'

'To live?'

'Yes, to be sure; you are my wife.'

'Haco, I cannot. I would be missed, and they would write my mother, and my father would come for me and it would be known.'

'But there's no use in our having got married, then.'

'It will be very nice to know that we are married, when people all round about us think we are nothing to each other.'

'Oh, that's nothing.'

While they conversed, the Sheriff who had united them looked closely into their names, saw who Haco was, and dashed off a little letter to an old friend of his own. It was:

'MY DEAR SIR THOMAS SPENS,—It has just occurred to me that I have allowed a boy and a girl to register themselves as man and wife, whom I ought to have delayed for further inquiries. Not that they are not legally married. They are, and so indisputably man and wife, that no man can put them asunder. I think it right, however, to say that the man is Haco Spens, your son, aged nineteen, and the wife—her hand shook so much I cannot make out the first word — something Baxter, daughter of Alexander Baxter, in your neighbourhood. Had I been more alert, I might have postponed this; under the circumstances, I can do nothing better than apprise you of what has occurred.

Haco and Tibbie parted on the Bridge.

CHAPTER XVI

THE PENNY GAFF

HACO felt exceedingly triumphant after he had got
married. It was a secret, and would remain so
from his father for years, it might be. In the
meantime, Sir Thomas would go on treating him as
a boy, whereas he was a man—a man of the world,
who might become an experienced, aged parent,
perhaps, in the course of time. Well, his father, he
reflected, had no business treating him with the
contempt he had poured upon him. He had liber-
ated him, his son, from all feeling of personal re-

sponsibility towards him. Not that he would not
cultivate such feelings of affection as a son ought
to entertain towards a father. He could do that ;
but he could not forgive him his nasty language,
and this decisive exercise of private judgment
consoled him. It was a great deal more to him
than passing high would have been at a degree
examination. He carried himself with the air
of a very superior person, indeed, as he sauntered across the Bridge after bidding his wife good-
bye. His wife! What a sound it had! To be
able to say to himself, 'My wife!' He paused, and
allowed himself to be elbowed to right and left by
people busier, or pretending to be busier, than himself, who passed backwards and forwards, while
he repeated the words, 'My wife! my wife.'

When he went back to Queen Street, Mrs
Ramsay came into his room, shut the door behind
her and said,

'Mr Spens, sir, when will you bring the lady home?'

'Very soon now, Mrs Ramsay; but there is a little diplomacy required. It may be a day or two, even a week or two; but, of course, I can't always go on away from my wife. I am married, you understand. Look at that.'

'Deary, deary, Mr Spens! and had you not a minister of the gospel to make the ceremony sacred?'

'No.'

'That was a pity. I could, for the price of a new hat, get a clergyman to come up and marry you according to the gospel.'

'He couldn't marry me any better than the Sheriff, could he? Look at that slip of paper.'

'Deary, deary!' said the landlady, going out in a state of deep mental anxiety about the girl who was to come and share her lucrative lodger's rooms.

She was not altogether displeased. She foresaw
a source of livelihood in it. She could bully this
young wife, if it were necessary. She could always
hold up before her the prospect of telling Mr Spens'
father—that is, should the young wife have a
critical eye upon the week's accounts. Being 'a
lady,' she was not likely to be very critical. In
any case, however, Mrs Ramsay was prepared for
her, and knew how to act.

In the afternoon Sandy looked up. He was surprised to observe that Haco received him with a
slight air of embarrassment. It passed off quickly
enough, and Haco offered him a cigar, which he
would not take.

'It creates a want,' said Sandy, 'and I can't afford
it.'

'Of course; so does anything you take that you
like create a want. I don't see how that can be
called an objection to it.'

'It's an objection to me, Spens, who haven't the same amount of money as you.'

'You are too careful, Sandy.'

'A person cannot be too careful. Economy, says Dominie Dunn, is the parent of all the virtues—of equity to one's neighbours, of independence, of cleanhandedness.'

'Oh! he has been quoting his copy-books to you.'

'Well, maybe he has; but if there's sagacity in a copy-book heading, I'm quite open to receive and digest it. Some wise man must have been at the back of it originally. But do you know, Spens, what I want you to do?'

'No.'

'This is a free night for both of us—no work to do—and I've never been at a place of amusement in my life. My father doesn't approve of it; but I'm taking my own line, and I have free orders to a gaff' down the Canongate.'

'Free orders to a gaff—worth twopence, I suppose.'

'I got them from a man who calls himself "The Great Snake." He's a queer character, and he promises to see that we are well seated, if we come.'

'Is he an actor in reduced circumstances?'

'He's a genius with a broken neck and joints, and can do anything with himself he likes, except break himself into little bits and come together again. There's no harm in the fellow either. He has taught me to dance, and I'm rather grateful to him. He'll be as proud as Punch if we go down and see him. There's somebody at the door.'

'Come in. Hillo! Tree, my dear fellow, you are very polite. Think of you knocking at the door!'

'Well, my young cock, how are you getting on? Who's this chap? I have not seen him before. He's an intelligent-looking chappie.'

'This is Baxter—Sandy Baxter, Tree, the ablest

man at the University. You have surely heard of
him ?'

'No, oddly enough, I have not. We don't hear
much of your great men under twenty years of
age, somehow. Yes, decidedly, I'll take one of
your cigars. I see you can smoke at last; it's an
accomplishment that it takes some little time to
learn. To learn it properly, you should begin at
ten years of age and prig your father's tobacco, if
you can get it. Do it when he is not looking, and
blame your little brother, if you have one. These
are the general principles of action I would lay
down to a rising generation which wanted to
become really accomplished puffers. But you are
past that time. You puff artistically. Now, what
are you boys up to? I want some amusement,
Spens, my boy—something of a harmless but in-
spiriting nature, which will not take away the
power of work to-morrow morning. You know
the town—the illimitable deeps of Edinburgh

Conduct me thither. Let me wander among them. Let me feel that I am invited, and that I am enjoying it.'

'Tree, you are just in time.'

'So?'

'Yes.'

'How's that? What have you discovered? A new pleasure?'

'Yes.'

'What?'

'A penny gaff, with free orders into it. We can all go in without paying at the door, and have the best seats in the house reserved for us. If that isn't a new pleasure, I don't know what you want or expect.'

'I don't want anything better. I thought at one time that painting Sir Thomas Spens in a rage would have been a new pleasure. Just to put him into a bit of canvas when he's raising his left arm and his throat gurgling into a truculent "Eh! eh!"

I thought that would be a new pleasure to the public, if I had him hung, to show how some men, when they make a little money, think it justifiable to abandon their manners—particularly if they think they are talking to a poor man. I'm sorry to say that about your father, Spens, but his " Eh! eh!" is an insult upon civilisation. If he had used that expression to me twice, he would have found his ancient nose inside my thumb and forefinger, and right well squeezed it would have been, notwithstanding his good luck and his fortune and his high old position—right well squeezed, Haco Spens. You should tell him about it—represent to him that it is an offence to men as well born as he is, if they haven't got his purse. I, Eli Tree, look back upon his " Eh! eh!" with contempt, and if I didn't think his son a jolly good fellow, I'd proceed to Binkie this very night and pull his venerable snout.'

'I say, Tree, you know you're too hard on the old man. He doesn't mean anything particular.'

'Why does he do it, then?'

'Why does he snore at night?'

'Because he can't help it, I suppose.'

'Very well, his "Eh? eh?" is exactly the same sort of thing. It doesn't mean anything.'

'It means, my young cock, a devouring egotism, a long abandonment of consideration for others, and a long concentration of consideration upon a sense of his own importance in the world—that's what it means.'

'Not a bit of it, Tree. It means that he has been always meeting blockheads who misunderstood him, and the manner he uses to blockheads, habitually, has stuck to him when he is addressing, a very different sort of fellow—namely, Eli Tree. I've heard him say "Eh? eh?" to Lord Farmline one of the touchiest of noblemen. He always says it to me. I've heard him say it to his microscope

at one o'clock in the morning, when he was looking
at bits of the eye. "Eh, eh," he would say, and he
would seem to wait and listen for an answer, and
none would come. Then he would sigh and shut
up his apparatus with a click. He's an aggravat-
ing man, my father; but don't you take it so
seriously, Tree. You opened a window one night,
within my experience, and pitched a ewerful of
water upon the heads of two elderly gentlemen.
That was worse than "Eh? eh?" People who live
in glass houses shouldn't, as Dominie Dunn would
say, throw stones—should they, Sandy?'

'No, I don't think they should.'

'Well, what about the gaff? Are you willing
to have a new pleasure, Tree?'

'I am.'

'There isn't an order for you, I'm afraid.'

'I have a pocketful of them,' said Sandy. 'I
lent him a two-shilling piece, fool that I was, and
he has given me these.'

'Better give them to me. I'll distribute them in the convalescent wards. They'll know how to use them.'

'Who is the performer?' asked Tree.

'The Great Snake.'

'Have you ever seen him, Spens?'

'No.'

'Very well, hats and coats on, and off to the penny gaff.'

The gaff was situated in a vacant space off the Canongate, where an enthusiastic Lord Provost had cleared away some historical houses which had become noisome through overcrowding. A century ago the space had rung to the jovial sounds of high people; to-night, however, they were very merry. On a platform, lit up by paraffin lamps, a girl in tights beat a drum, while a skeleton danced a lively dance of death. The head of a good-looking woman was visible at a little window taking coppers, her attention being divided between that and a plate of steak, which she devoured with an enjoyment appreciated by a rude crowd outside, who had not dined quite so well.

'That's the Snake,' said Sandy, as Tree, Haco and he elbowed their way through the crowd, and stood, under the beating of the drum, in the light of the lamps.

Dum! dum! dum! dum! went the drumsticks, as Sandy's friend made one or two of his less important movements to attract the crowd.

'I have seen that man before,' said Haco.

'That's what I said the first time I saw him,' remarked Sandy.

'Come along with your orders,' roared Tree, making room for himself with his elbow in a highly rude and aggressive manner. 'I never had an order at a gaff before. I hope it's a box seat.'

He led the way up the rickety wooden steps

where the skeleton was performing, and, standing on the platform, waited for Haco and Sandy.

Sandy however had mislaid the orders. He couldn't find them. He searched his pockets, and drew out nothing but a handkerchief. The Snake approached the edge of the platform, while the dum! dum! dum! dum! went on, and, opening his mouth, he leant over and gaped.

The crowd laughed. Tree posed as if he were a hired assassin.

'Bloodless Bone,' he shouted, drawing an imaginary dagger from beneath a Highland tippet —'Bloodless Bone, you will oblige me by passing us free to box seats—these gentlemen and myself.'

Haco at that moment came up with a handful of coppers in lieu of orders. Sandy followed slowly, still feeling his pockets. The Snake took the coppers, advanced to the light of a lamp, tossed them in the air, seemed to swallow, digest, and evacuate them in three rapid movements.

'By my halidom, I will fillip thee on the nose, '
said Tree, 'with my small pinkey, if thou dost not
pass us without the adventitious aid of coppers.'

The Skeleton walked along the platform, performing everything he could do in succession, and,
standing before Tree, said,

'Pass friend.'

From Haco, however, he took a penny, and
Sandy showing no ticket, he ignored his friendship,
and looked cold till he had been paid the entry-
money to the show.

They went in, and saw a sawdust ring and an
intelligent pony going round smelling for biscuits
from the people at the edge.

'A box seat!' shouted Tree. 'By my halidom,
a box seat, or beshrew me, I will bethink myself of
a r-r-r-r-e-e-e-venge!'

A small boy in white tights and spangles took
them to a seat by themselves, and they sat down
waiting.

Dum! dum! dum! dum! went the drumstick outside. The people inspired by Tree's example, crowded in. Benches filled up, and presently a corpse was brought in upon a stage-table.

CHAPTER XVII

APPREHENSION

THE corpse had no sooner been laid on the table than Haco burst out with an exclamation of horror.

'By jingo!' said Tree, 'this is acting—real acting! That fellow looks as dead as a door-nail. But he has died too soon, hasn't he? To judge from the chap with the towel in his hand, he shouldn't die till the chloroform is applied. It's a tableau from the hospital—very well arranged, too. But they might have got a better surgeon

than that seedy youth standing round, not knowing what to do. That's the Great Snake on the
table. I must have that fellow up to my studio
and smoke a pipe with him. There are ideas in
him.'

'Spens, you are looking awfully ill,' said Sandy,
looking at Haco, who had covered his face with
his hand.

'I am ill,' murmured Haco. 'Everybody knows
it. They are putting me on the stage. I am infamous. I am a known murderer. Tree, let me
out; I must leave this den.'

'Sit down, will you, Spens? you haven't seen the
end of the scene. You don't know what it's coming to. What are you jabbering about?'

He pushed Spens into his place with his elbow,
and the scene proceeded. The corpse on the operating-table had a towel applied to its head; but
instead of becoming more inanimate, it gradually
rose and commenced a rotatory motion with its

right leg; it performed half-a-dozen movements like a wheel in circuit, upon the table; it broke its back and leapt high into the air, landing among the sawdust, arms akimbo.

'I say though,' murmured Sandy. 'I seem to recollect now where I saw the Snake first of all. This parody on an operation is a refresher. I believe I'm not wrong in recollecting that the Snake was that very man on the operating-table which poor Spens thinks he killed. Spens,' he added, in a whisper, 'sit it out with your friend, and I'll be back in a few minutes.'

In a few minutes he returned with his friend, Robert, the bobby, who was in plain clothes, but who seemed to have something in his coat-pocket of a massive description. They sat down quietly behind Tree and Haco, and were in time to hear the latter describe the persecution he had been enduring for a year, owing to the incident in the hospital.

'God bless me, Spens! why didn't you tell me this before?'

'I wanted to say as little about it as possible. It seemed to me always better to pay than to secure publicity and become infamous. But, you see, I am infamous in any case.'

'And this Roger fellow, where does he hang out?'

'Up the Canongate a little.'

'Very well, then; as soon as the performance is over.—The Snake's an artist, and can't be interrupted at his work.—As soon as the performance is finished we'll go and see Roger, and take the Snake with us; and see if I don't make him swallow a bottle of his own castor oil. Will that satisfy you?'

'It won't clear the debt to the widow and orphans.'

'Widow and orphans, you simpleton; there are no widow and orphans, if I make out your story right.'

'Mr Tree,' said Sandy, who had been listening, bending towards him from behind, 'here's an old friend. Do you recognise him?'

Tree, who never forgot a face he once saw, looked round.

'Do I recognise him? Yes. It's the bobby who did me a service one night at Christie's. How d'ye do, bobby? I hope you're very well. D'ye want to nab anybody?'

'Whisht!' said Sandy.

'You do want to nab somebody?'

'I want him to nab the Snake.'

'What! nab the man who gave you free orders to the gaff? Not if I know it. Besides, if I make this story out, the Snake isn't the culprit at all. It's Roger, the man in the ally with the LL.D., who is to blame and who must be punished.'

Spens expostulated, and said he would rather the thing remained out of sight. He would prefer them to do nothing. He was content to remain infamous.

'The infamy doesn't matter that,' said Tree, snapping his thumb violently; 'but the two pounds a-week matter a good deal. Don't you say it doesn't, Spens. It may get you into such a crop of trouble as your best efforts, or the efforts of your friends, won't be able to take you out of, and the trouble keeps springing up, rank, luxuriant, here, there, and everywhere, all over the field.'

They sat for a few minutes, till a new tableau was brought to the sawdust. Then Tree said,

'I think we may go behind the scenes now, where the canvas is flapping. I saw the Snake go in there. But, bobby, and intelligent-looking chappie, don't you come yet. Wait till you're called for.'

Tree disappeared at a corner where the wind was flapping the canvas.

It was a sort of retiring-room. The Snake was

standing in it, with a hunk of cheese and a pot of
porter. He bowed when he saw Tree, and made
one of his outrageous movements with his leg. He
did not know Haco from Adam, and only scrutinized
him to see if he were likely to be worth a treat.

Tree was a little staggered at that. He thought
if he were the veritable man of the hospital tragedy,
he would probably have recognized Haco. However, he assumed that he was the man.

'Now, look here, Snake,' he said, 'you've played
this game too long. You've been going halves in
the plunder of Dr Roger.'

'Which I hain't,' said the Snake. 'Wishes I 'ad.
Half o' Dr Roger's plunder means a big haul.
He's making shillings like a mint—never stops
from mornin' till night, he don't.'

'You know what I mean, Snake.'

'Which I don't, with your leave.'

Tree seized him by the throat, and he could not
wriggle out of his grasp, though he dropped his pot

and made extensive dislocations of arms, legs, and back-bone.

'It's no use,' said Tree. 'You know precious well you are the man this young gentleman thought he choked off with chloroform in the infirmary waiting-room about a year ago. D'ye hear me?'

'Oh, *that!*' said the Snake. 'That's no source o' income to me—barrin' a little liquorice-stick and tamarind-water when I call upon my medical adviser. Barrin' that and a odd shillin', I get nothin' for that job.'

'You don't?'

'No, not I. And, now I recognise you, you *are* the young person I let in for a practical joke. Yes, I ain't goin' to deny it now it's found out. But, lor! what is it to a baronite's son?—a shillin' or two a-week to a wet cove like me. You wouldn't miss it.'

'You really are,' said Haco, raising the flapping

canvas—'you are the man who was lying on that table?'

'In course I are. I ain't a-going to deny it, now I'm found out. I are.'

'God bless you!' said Haco.

'Thank ye,' said the Snake, looking at Tree.

'He's glad you're alive, you ruffian.'

'He has a forgivin' spirit.'

'Yes; happily for you, he has. But, Snake, you will lead the way to the medical adviser's, and I'll call two of my friends down from their box seat.'

Tree put his head inside and wagged two fore-fingers at Sandy and the policeman. They walked down and went out by a back way from the gaff, Tree keeping pace with Snake, the rest following. They were not long in arriving at the mouth of the slum where the shop was. It was full of people at the time—Roger, with his smoking-cap on, weighing and scooping and tying and waxing in the deftest manner. He was evidently dosing the whole neighbourhood, with the most lucrative results. The party waited outside till the shop emptied ; then they went in.

'Doctor Thorburn,' said Tree, with an agitated expression. But it was no use his attempting to pass himself off as a patient. He was too rubicund and healthy. Besides, Roger saw that the party were hostile, from the expression in the eye of the Snake. Nevertheless, he politely invited them to come into his parlour, and they went.

'Now, sir,' said Tree, 'you see this young gentleman ? '

'I do.'

'You see this disjointed animal who calls himself the Great Snake ? '

'I know the Great Snake personally. He is a very good friend of mine. Take a chair, Snake. After they are gone we can have some toasted cheese.'

'Some toasted cheese!' said Tree. 'Will you, though?'

'I hope so. Now, gentlemen, what can I do for you?'

'Go down on your knees and beg this young gentleman's pardon.'

'Hardly.'

'Down, you dog!' And Tree, seizing him, forced him roughly on his haunches, from which he jerked him forward on his knees.

'Ask his pardon this minute, you pill-box, you— you blue bottle of cold-drawn castor oil—you ounce of assafœtida, you!' Roger struggled, but Tree held him in position. 'Stand forward, Snake. Is it true that you agreed to go to the waiting-room table for a sixpenny wager, acting a death as a "do" upon a green house-surgeon?'

'It is.'

'Is it true that this decocter of nastiness kept up the joke, and made a purse of it?'

'It is.'

'Did he pay you in proportion to your share?'

'No.'

'What did he give you?'

'First five shillings, then four, then three, then two, then one, then a sixpence a-week. Last week only liquorice-stick.'

'And he wants to bribe you to-night with a bit of toasted cheese! Down dog! Spens you said something about a certificate of death. Where is it, you bottle-stopper, you stick of sealing-wax, you coil of thin blue string?'

'I know the drawer,' said the Snake.

'Fetch it out. Policeman in plain clothes, take out your handcuffs.'

The handcuffs were brought out, and Roger's struggles ceased at that point. The Snake found the false certificate, and Sandy, looking at it, said,

'The form is right enough, but the filling up is a fraud. He might get ten years for this.'

'What do you say to that?—eh, to that, you Gregory's mixture, you—you black draught, you grovelling colocynthe, you fraudulent pills and ointment! You say nothing to it. But what do you think of the year of torture you have given to this boy? Speak will you?'

Roger was in no humour to speak. Indeed Tree held him down with so violent a hand that it was difficult for him to compass language.

Haco began to be a little sorry for the man. He interceded for him, and said 'that after all, he was very pleased to find there had been no death.'

'No, no, my young cock, that won't do. You clear out and fetch a cab. You'll find one, most likely, under the Tron Church.'

Haco went as he was directed.

'Now he's gone, and before we take this doser off to cooler quarters than he has here, he must swallow one of his own boluses. Snake, fetch me a bottle of cold-drawn castor oil. Mix a package of salts, and set that electrical apparatus in order ; we want them all. Hold his legs—hold him bobby. Now keep his mouth open and pass the bottle.'

In a twinkling Tree had the battery working at high-pressure, the castor oil descending in a deluge at his throat, and the salts, warmed with water from the hob, to top up with.

When Haco came in from the Tron, saying he had brought a cab, he saw Roger on the floor, a greasy and dishevelled wretch, whose moans were pitiful to hear. But Tree was inexorable.

'Now shove him into a blanket, carry him to the cab, and at the bottom of my studio you will find a coal cellar, warranted to contain five-and-forty rats any night. He will remain there, hand-cuffed, for further orders from the dustman.'

The doctor was carried out in the blanket and driven to his dungeon, into which he was bundled, without a single accompaniment, save a parting kick from Tree.

CHAPTER XVIII

THE END

IT was not till the following day that Haco felt the profound relief of not being a murderer by accident. He was really rather sorry for the sneak who had kept up the delusion on him so long, though he did not follow him to the dungeon where Tree temporarily confined him.

'I don't believe in law,' said Tree, after it was all over. 'I think, where a fellow of that sort is concerned, law is wasted on him. Hang me if justice hasn't overtaken him in the only form he

can understand it. He shall have another bottle
of castor oil to-morrow and a bit of dog-biscuit.
Then I'll kick him out. He's sure to blunder
into the hands of the hangman, sooner or later.
Thank goodness for that!'

So ended an episode which had ruined Haco's
year. He now looked forward to a new period.
Again he thought of his wife, and with pleasure,
that he could now have all his allowance to himself.
She would be able to save it for him, and apply it,
and look after it. It really was very jolly, he
thought, to find what good luck his marriage had
already brought him—the good luck of an exposure
of a cad who had been worrying him to death,
and that without any very absurd publicity. He
intended now that medicine should become attractive for him ; that it should be more his aim in life
than boating and desultory reading, and long walks
by moonlight and sails on the Firth. His little
wife would help him to take an earnest view of it,

he was assured. She would encourage him to get
first-class certificates. She would inspire him in a
thousand ways unknown to any other body, and
the end of it would be that, with an honourable
degree, his father would be very glad to extend a
cordial hand to her. To be sure, many vexatious
things might occur in the meantime; how, for
example, to keep the marriage from Mr Baxter's
ears and avert his anger, but he trusted to Mrs
Baxter being on his side, as she always was,
especially when he was paying attentions to Tibbie.

He was standing in his room, with his coat off,
dusting his books, when he heard at his back the
familiar sound of ' Bonnie Mary Hay, it's a holiday
to me,' and, much to his surprise, he found himself,
presently, face to face with Professor Stewart.

' Welcome, professor, to my rooms. I consider
this a very great honour. Indeed I do.'

' You're welcome to it. I wish I was young
enough to feel anything an honour. At my time, a

sweet nap or a successful meal is more than any
honour. Ah, the illusions of boyhood! If you
only knew it, man, it's better to be a boy like you
than an aged gentleman like me, at the top of the
tree—a hundred times better, and you should be
thankful for it. Dignity has its advantages; but
what compensation is it for the loss of youth?
Don't you pray to become a curmudgeon before
your time. Go out in the sunlight, fall in love,
write poems about it, play the fool, and when you
have come to my time of life, you'll look back on
it all and say, " Then I was wise." But that's not
what I meant to say : that's not what I came here
about. It struck me forcibly the other day that
you're not the man for the Blue Pill Society. You
belong to us—to us of the " Hellenic." Come over
there and hear us read a garbled chorus, and see
what you can do at it, and if you can't do anything,
look like a Greek.'

'I can try to do that, of course,' said Haco: and

that moment his door opened, and his father came in, wearing an evil expression on his face.

He saw Haco, with his jacket off, speaking to Professor Stewart. He had expected to find him dandling his new wife. It slightly allayed his wrath. Nor could he afford to be beside himself, with the professor in the room.

'Father!' said Haco, suddenly remembering, at the sight of him, that he was in his shirt-sleeves.

Sir Thomas gave a snort of contempt, declined to shake hands with him, bowed to Professor Stewart, and sat down.

'Spens,' said the professor, 'I haven't seen you since that archæological rout at Farmline. You're grumpier than ever. If I had a son like this, I would shake hands with him when I met him.'

'Would you?'

'Decidedly.'

'That might depend upon circumstances.'

'Do you mean that he's not worthy of having

his hand shaken by venerable and innocent gentlemen like you and me ?'

'I have taught him to respect old age, Professor
Stewart.'

'What bit of it did you ask him to bow down to
most—the crooked knees, or the gray hairs, or the
wheezy chest—eh ?'

'To the experience that it brings.'

'Ay, that's all very well and does it never bring
vanity and avarice, and dodginess and politic arts ?'

'D—— it, Stewart, peruse that, will you, and cease
your insinuations against wisdom and influence and
the capacity to guide youth to its proper destiny.'

'Well, you've put him into the Blue Pill Society.
I don't call that guiding a young poet to his
destiny. Eh ? What ? You don't say so ? What !
Married ! Save the young man ! Married ! Spens,
my young friend, *dulce est desipere*, but this is too
much of a good thing !'

Haco shrank to the further end of the room and

looked out at the window. He could not conceive how he had been discovered. At the moment he felt greatly inclined to lift the window and vault into the street.

'I have come to the conclusion that he has no cerebrum,' said Sir Thomas; 'that he is an irresponsible being; that he has no '——

'Then you are quite wrong. You have entirely misread your lad, and, I'm bound to say, in making this revelation, I think you have misdirected him in sending him here. My dear sir, our old Scotch Universities are all very well for a certain order of natures—natures that are hardy and tough and prepared to fight the battle of life, trampling on other men's toes, digging them in the ribs, knocking them down, where that is needful; it is absolutely and totally unfit for Haco and such as he. You understand my quarrel with Oxford, Sir Thomas? Very well, you will not misunderstand me when I say that to Oxford that lad should have been sent. There he will come to maturity with perfect safety; here there are unnumbered pitfalls.'

'The fool is a married man.'

'Yes,' said Haco, suddenly wheeling round and confronting the old gentleman—'yes, father, I admit it. But I have not taken home my wife yet. I parted with her on the Bridge, and have not seen her since. Let me ask your forgiveness, and then I shall introduce you to one of the simplest, most frugal, most innocent girls in the world, just such a one as will save my income for me and help me towards my degree.'

'Prettily pled, youngster,' said Professor Stewart.

'Go on,' said Sir Thomas.

'I will introduce you to Tibbie Baxter.'

'To whom?'

'To the girl who was reaping in the field with me one night, when you looked over.'

Sir Thomas had expected worse tidings. He expected to hear that it was the lad's landlady's elderly, ugly daughter, In his experience he had known of a few being palmed off upon susceptible students in their first year. He looked pitifully at Professor Stewart, however, as he remarked :

'He has married the daughter of my grieve.'

'And how old do you say she is ? '

'Not yet nineteen.'

'Humph ! '

'Humph ! '

'She is the best of girls; she is the gentlest; she is not absolutely beautiful, but she is beautiful enough '——

'Hold, sir' said Sir Thomas. 'Are you willing to go to Oxford and study for a degree ? '

'Certainly, father.'

'Very good. To Oxford you shall go. And this young female '——

'My wife, father.'

'And this wife of yours shall keep my house for

the next month. She will then go to a boarding-school in Switzerland, and, if you have behaved yourself in the interval, you may live with her in your twenty-fourth year, with my consent. Attempt it before you have an English degree, and you are no longer my son.'

'It's a fair offer,' said Professor Stewart.

'I accept it,' murmured Haco.

THE END

www.ingramcontent.com/pod-product-compliance
Lightning Source LLC
Chambersburg PA
CBHW031422020726
47499CB00005B/1550